#1 London Screaming

Written by K.B. Brege
Illustrated by D. Brege

This book is a work of fiction. All names, characters, places, and incidents are either products of the author's wild imagination, invented or used fictitiously. Ghosts however, may exist.

ISBN 13: 978-09774119-6-2
ISBN 10: 0-9774119-6-6

The trademark Ghost Board Posse® is registered in the U.S. Patent and Trademark Office.
Printed in the United States of America
First Printing Paperback edition – June 2008

Copyediting by Janice Pollard. Email: pollard_jan@yahoo.com

Skateboard trick consultation by Josh Knepper.
www.joshknepper.com

Be safe! Always wear a helmet when participating in any extreme sports!

Acknowledgements

An unbelievably huge thank you goes out to Darrin Brege and Mick Brege who inspire me with their undisputed love for the paranormal and all things scary.

Also, a big thank you to Josh Knepper, a talented professional boarder who has been my consultant on anything that has to do with the actual aspect of skateboarding. I give my heartfelt thanks to him for all of his help on the names and descriptions of each and every skateboard trick – which are real and not fiction.

One
Twickenshire, England

It was nearing midnight in the village of Twickenshire. The annual ritual began as the townspeople boarded up their windows, closed their shutters and locked the doors to their homes and businesses. The village, which was about 45 minutes north of London, was normally a bustling town -- full of life on any Friday night. But this was not just any Friday night. It was the eve of the 250th anniversary of the ghastly murder at the Castle Cloon de Sade. One of the most heinous crimes in England, one that left an indelible mark on the village for hundreds of years that could never be erased. The thought of it still haunts every person who lives in Twickenshire.

"Alrighty then, time to go. May we pay our tab?" asked the vibrant young Englishman wearing casual clothes and a baseball cap with a ghost insignia on it. He was standing at the hand-carved wood bar, in the small, cozy stone and thatch pub with two other men wearing identical caps.

Emily, an attractive athletic-looking girl with long dark hair and striking eyes stopped wiping the counter. She

1

slowly pulled the bill of the last customers' out of her small red apron. She had enjoyed chatting with the fellows; ironically, they had similar interests to her own. Yet, even though she had researched the Castle Cloon de Sade extensively, she never had any desire to go there, and knew no one should. It wasn't her place to say anything to them, but she felt she had to say something.

"You're *not* really going to go up there, are you?" She boldly asked the three men in front of her.

Surprised at her nerve, they just stared at her.

Without missing a beat, she pointed out towards their equipment truck. "I mean I know you consider yourself experts in the field of ghost hunting and all, but those fancy devices and that expensive equipment will do you no good in that castle!"

"Emily," said Derek, the pub owner, who had overheard her.

"No, really. Just how many castles have you investigated?" She insisted.

"Emily!"

"…And regardless, it doesn't matter, because I can personally tell you I know there is not one place on this planet as haunted or evil as the Castle Cloon de Sade."

"Emily, it's none of your business!" Derek scowled.

Emily stood there silently for a moment but still couldn't hold back…

2

"I've heard personal accounts of what has happened to some of the lucky few who have made it out of the castle alive!"

Except for the crackling in the fireplace, an eerie silence filled the small pub.

"And none of it was worth their curiosity," Emily continued in a somber tone. "One was so horrified that the whites of his eyes were all that shone – no iris, no pupil and, as far as I know, he could never see again. Another had the initials C.C.D.S. carved into his blood-drenched clothes and on his cheeks and he walked with arms outstretched – mummified! And did you ever hear of the S.O.S., the Society of Spirits? Their bodies, men and women alike, were found at the bottom of the hill in pieces! Need I say more?"

"If it's any consolation…see this tattoo?" asked one of the ghost hunters.

Emily slowly turned her head to look at the man as he yanked his customized t-shirt up over his shoulder.

She slowly nodded her head.

"Can you read it for me?" he asked her gruffly.

"G R A T E F U L like me," Emily read.

"Right-o, Ms. Em, but do you know what that really stands for?"

Emily shook her head no.

Ghosts…Rarely…Are…Trouble…Even…For…

3

<u>Ug</u>ly…<u>L</u>oafs like me!" he stated and began to laugh.

Within minutes, everyone had joined in on the laughter, except Emily. She stood silently staring at them. The ghost hunters once again reassured her they would be fine, while picking up their backpacks filled with EMF detectors and recorders. They continued to explain that they were professionals, and that nothing bad had ever happened to them. How most supposedly haunted places turned out to be nothing but vicious rumors. They were certain time had exaggerated what happened at the Castle Cloon de Sade.

But Emily Tibley knew better. Even though she was a newcomer to Twickenshire; she wasn't a stranger. She had moved there recently from South Hampton, but her ancestors had originated from the village.

As an aspiring writer, she had decided to do a book on what really happened at the wickedly haunted castle.

While working part time at the pub, she interviewed many of the local families. Like her, their ancestors had also been brutalized by the original owner of the castle, the evil, vicious Duke Gregario Cloon de Sade.

Emily had listened to the countless stories about the horrible castle's past owners, as well as local gossip about people who had tried to venture into the castle – and never ever came out. And how the few who did were never the same again – what she feared most for the ghost hunters. She stared out of the pub's window watching, as the ghost

4

hunters' truck pulled away, then turned to go up the road toward the castle.

Although Emily had acquired quite a bit of material for her book since moving to Twickenshire, there was one thing missing -- the most important part...What really did happen 250 years ago?

Two
Harlo King, Ocean City, Maryland

The boarding competition was only two days away and Harlo King had one thing on his mind – winning! The thing he loved to do best was ride boards -- skateboards, snowboards and surfboards. His second favorite thing to do was surfing – the Internet.

Harlo, an average 16 year old with a friendly personality, had become completely entranced with the paranormal online. The thought of ghosts and haunted places completely fascinated him.

It all started when he bought a laptop with the money he had saved working at his parents' restaurant. A friend had forwarded him a link to an expert on supernatural occurrences. Harlo had communicated with the expert – who went by the name of Ghost Talker (GT) on instant message. They developed a friendship based on their keen interest in the paranormal. So much so, that sometimes Harlo found it hard to pull himself away from the Internet to pursue his boarding.

But today was a different story. It was summer break and he had only one day left to get his routine together for the Thrash Energy Drink Contest on the boardwalk. He knew this particular competition would be fierce. This was the one that would separate the amateurs from the pros, and Harlo was determined to become a pro. But to do that he needed a sponsor. This was his big chance.

He pushed his curly brown hair away from his face as he signed off from GT with a "ttyl." Until the competition was over, Harlo decided to do nothing except practice his boarding.

He grabbed his skateboard and headed downstairs.

"And just exactly what is that in your hand?" asked his mother when he reached the landing of the small wooden steps.

"Oh, this? This is a skateboard, I believe," he retorted as a sly smile revealed his silver braces.

"Don't be smart. I'm the only one in this house who can be smart. Anyway, I don't think so…Your dad is expecting you at the restaurant."

"But mom! Moooommmm! Tomorrow is the Thrash Energy Drink Contest! You know the one put on by Sisu Soda, the one that I, Harlo King, am gonna be king of!"

"The only king that you're going to be is king of your room when your dad grounds you for not showing up!" His mom stated, while picking up her purse and the box of newly printed menus off the kitchen table. "If you don't come with me right now to help us get ready to open for the season, I guarantee you can kiss that contest goodbye! Besides, at 16, you're lucky we're even letting you enter!"

"Can't Jeff help at the restaurant?" Harlo moaned.

"For your information, your brother has been at the restaurant since early this morning! Now you know this family works together. Chop chop!"

Harlo frowned and nodded. He glumly followed his mother out the front door. The rickety screen creaked and slammed shut behind him.

Harlo could smell the fresh sea-salt air and winced in the bright sunlight. He descended down the worn wooden steps with flaking paint that stood in front of the dingy blue and white Cape Cod home. The house had been in his family for years, passed down from his great-grandfather. It was the same thing with the family restaurant - King's Crab Shack. He despised the restaurant because he had to work there every summer since he could remember. Maybe it was his family's dream to live in a seasonal seaside town and run a crab shack for rich visiting tourists, but not his. Harlo had bigger plans.

Three
Donell James, Detroit, Michigan

"You stink!" yelled Andre.

"Yeah...*ha, ha, ha.* You do!" laughed Keyshawn.

"Why? Why do I stink? Just cuz I didn't make it around the curve? The same curve that both of you two idiots just fell off of?" snapped Donell as he got up and brushed off his torn jeans. He pulled his t-shirt down, picked up his skateboard and began to walk down the marble steps in front of the huge office building.

"Hey, man, where you going?" asked Andre, "I was just jokin' with you. It's time to ride!"

"I'm sick of you two doggin' me!" said Donell.

"Puh-leez...you know you're better than us...you stupid dreadlock wearin' homeboy."

"What did you say?" asked Donell, stopping frozen in his tracks. He put his skateboard down, hit it with his foot, then just as the skateboard popped up in the air, he flipped it over with his other foot, jumped on it and pulled a front side 180 no comply.

Andre and Keyshawn immediately broke into a round of applause as Donell followed his smooth move with a Casper to 360 half flip.

9

"I'm down with that!" yelled Andre.

Donell was the best skateboarder of the three of them, and they knew it. His moves were effortless. Since he was tall and thin, when he skated, he made it look like he was floating.

The three friends had big plans to enter and win the Thrash Energy Drink Contest on Saturday. But Andre and Keyshawn knew in their hearts that Donell would take first place.

Donell James lived in Detroit all his life. He came from a large family with two brothers and two sisters. His father, a factory worker for an automotive company, worked hard to provide for his family. He had a better life in mind for his children. He wanted each one of them to attend college, something he and his wife hadn't been fortunate enough to do.

Since Donell was the oldest, they were counting on him to set an example. His father knew if Donell applied himself, he could get a college scholarship for basketball. Little did he know, when Donell said he was out playing basketball with friends, he was really boarding in the city.

Donell and his two best friends honed their skills, as Detroit offered them plenty of challenges. It was a far cry from the everyday suburban skateboard parks. They would grind rails and ride down everything from marble steps in front of glossy modern buildings, to old iron ladders around trash cans in graffiti-filled back alleys. They would challenge each other as they watched their moves in mirrored plate glass windows.

As much fun as it was, Donell was serious about skateboarding. He knew Saturday's grand prize money would be enough to help his family. Plus, the scholarship would cover his first two years of college. He knew he had to win.

Four
Freddy Palamau, Kauai, Hawaii

'RIIINNNNGGGG RIIINNNNGGG!' Freddy Palamau kept hitting it over and over again – but for some reason his alarm clock would not stop ringing. Until he realized it wasn't his alarm that he was hitting, it was his phone.

"Aloha…it's your Pal," Freddy said groggily into the phone.

"Yo! Dude! Surf's up!" said an excited voice on the other end. "See you in fifteen at the pier, and have I got a surprise for you!"

"Uhhh…okay. Great. Who is this?" questioned Freddy.

"Dude…it's John Travolta. Who do you think it is?!" asked his best friend Steven.

"Awww, I knew it was you all along, I saw you in Hairspray. Man did you look weird…" laughed Freddy as he rolled out of bed and slid into his flip flops.

"Ha, ha! Very funny! Be there in fifteen," said Steven.

"No problemo," said Freddy.

Freddy Palamau, known to everyone as 'Pal,' was one of the friendliest and funniest kids in Kauai. Short, stocky, with medium length wavy black hair that was always pulled neatly back in a ponytail, he loved to eat and was always full of energy. Except for today, he was extremely tired.

The day before, his family had thrown him an enormous graduation party. Pal had graduated from high school a year early and with honors. He worked hard to do so. Pal had planned on spending the rest of his life surfing, while gradually taking over his parents' business. The Palamau family owned a chain of souvenir stores and a hotel. If Pal wasn't surfing, he was flirting with one of the 'fair haired maidens' as he liked to call the tourist girls that would wander into their stores.

He loved Kauai and always referred to it as "the most beautiful place on earth." It was always the perfect temperature. There were beautiful landscapes everywhere; from pristine beaches to stunning cliffs, mysterious caves to breathtaking waterfalls. Pal vowed he would never leave.

He grabbed his gear and headed down the enormous curving staircase of his parents' massive home. He chuckled as he glanced up at the hundreds of neon colored balloons that lined the ceiling from the party the night before.

"Can I make you breakfast Pal-Freddy?" asked the maid while cleaning up.

13

"No, thank you, Lalena! Surf's up and this kahuna's going to ride!" he winked.

As he strolled through the kitchen, he grabbed two giant blueberry muffins and headed into the garage. He quickly ate one of the muffins and stuffed the other one into the front pocket of his bright Hawaiian shirt.

After strapping on his helmet, he jumped onto his electric scooter while thinking about how relaxing this summer was going to be. The scooter curved around the enormous driveway and through the massive iron gates down the beach road.

When he got to the local hangout at the pier, his friend Steven came running up to him. Steven and Pal had been friends since elementary school.

"Aloha...ahhh, another beautiful day in Kauai!" said Pal looking up as he stretched his arms out.

"Yeah, aloha. Dude! You are like not gonna believe this! Come with me!"

Pal followed Steven through the sand to the hamburger joint where Steven worked. On the side of the small white building there were always all sorts of posters and flyers about upcoming events on the island.

"Look!" yelled Steven with delight as he pointed.

Pal stared at the countless flyers covering the side of the building.

"Can you believe it bro?" asked Steven.

"No, I can't," stated Pal.

"Well, what do you think?" asked Steven.

"I think it's disgusting!" answered Pal.

"Disgusting?" asked Steven wrinkling his brow confused.

"Yeah, you should clean this mess up."

"Not that! This!" Steven yelled excitedly while pounding his finger on a big glossy poster.

Pal moved closer to read it.

Sisu Soda's Thrash Energy Drink was holding its first contest for sponsorship. There was a huge grand prize, plus scholarship money and a worldwide tour. The contest would be held in four places: Detroit, Michigan; Ocean City, Maryland; Kapaa, Kauai; and Venice Beach, California.

They were looking for 16-18-year-old amateur skate boarders to sponsor who were ready to go pro. It was the first time a competition like this was held, because part of it would be how well their skills went from one boarding sport to another. If they were excellent skaters, later on in the tour they would have to prove their skills at surfing, snowboarding and mountain boarding. The poster read **'Challenge Yourself Because You'll Be Challenged!'**

"Why do you suppose they picked Detroit? It's the only place that doesn't have an ocean," questioned Pal casually while picking up his surfboard and moving toward the glistening blue ocean.

"I dunno," answered Steven as he pondered Pal's question for a moment, "They do have the Great Lakes...Dude! Never mind about geography! That's not

16

why I showed it to you. I showed it to you because you have to enter!"

"Look, bro, I think you've been spending entirely too much time in the sun," Pal replied seriously as he stopped to look at Steven.

"C'mon, Pal, you'll win! Do it for the boarders of Kauai! You know you're off the hook when it comes to boarding!" pleaded Steven.

"Right, surfboards. Not skateboards! This model physique will shatter a skateboard and bend those tiny little wheels in seconds!" laughed Pal as he made a huge curving motion of a board bending with his hands.

"No way, dude, I can prove that if you can surf, you can skate!" said Steven as he pulled a brand new skateboard out of his backpack and shoved it at Pal. "Besides, just how do you think skateboarding was invented? Huh? I'll tell you, bro, surfers invented skateboarding when there were no waves to surf on!"

"No way, bro!" stated Pal questioningly.

"Way!"

In the course of five minutes, Pal's life plans had changed.

17

Five
Terrence Zevon, Barstow, California

The ancient window air conditioner whirred and clacked as if it was dying, while barely cooling the cramped, messy trailer.

Terrence Zevon stood in the tiny kitchen trying to be as quiet as possible while he scrambled eggs over a hotplate. It was all they had to cook with since the gas had been turned off.

But today it didn't matter to him. Today he was energized. This was the one day he wouldn't have to worry about the bills, or about straightening up the messy trailer again. Nor would he have to sweat at his job on the ranch in the sweltering Barstow temperatures.

Barstow was a small railroad town with a military base near the Mojave Desert. There wasn't much to do there and Terrence longed for the excitement of a big city. He knew today could change everything for him.

At 18 years old he had model good looks; the picture perfect blond California boy with a muscular frame, perfect skin, super white teeth and long shiny sun-bleached blond hair. But despite his handsome appearance, there was a sad, dark side to his life.

18

CRRRAAAASSSHHH!!! One of the dirty glasses from the pile lining the sink fell to the floor.

"Terrrryyy! I am trying to sleep!" whined his mother from the other room.

Terrence, as he liked to refer to himself, shook his head as he turned off the hotplate. He scooped up the broken glass in an old newspaper and threw it away. He quickly sat down at the small rickety table to eat. He knew he'd have to scarf down his food in order to escape seeing his mother.

This was the one day he didn't have time for her negativity and defeatist attitude. Sometimes he felt sorry for her, but usually he just felt sick to his stomach that she didn't care enough to change her life.

She blamed everything in the world on why she was broke, alone…always complaining. She failed to look at the fact that she had him, a son, who had always stood by her side. He even dropped out of high school two years early to get a job and support her, and he had liked school. It was something he really regretted. But he knew in his heart that if he could win this contest, he could finish high school and go to college.

Even after giving up so much for his mother, nothing had changed. The sad fact was that she was still young. If she would just let the past go and find a job, she could have a decent life.

Terrence unfolded the flyer he kept hidden in his jeans pocket and read it for the zillionth time. When he originally came across it, he wasn't sure if he should enter the contest or not, but decided it was a once-in-a-lifetime chance.

When he wasn't working at the ranch, he would mountain board. He had gotten so good at it that he could board off the side of a barn and land on a makeshift ramp with barely a wobble. He knew he was exceptional at boarding. Sometimes he would board to the closest town with a skateboard park, since there wasn't one in Barstow.

The bedroom door creaked open.

"Whad'ya doin'?" asked a groggy voice as his mother tottered out of the room. Her disheveled curly blonde hair fell in her eyes as she reached for a cigarette.

Startled, Terrence quickly folded the flyer and stuffed it back in his pocket while shoveling the last bite of eggs into his mouth.

"Just…just havin' some breakfast," He stammered.

"Yeah, what were you reading?" she asked moving unsteadily to the table.

"Oh. Uh…I saw an ad for…for a job," He replied.

"Oh, really? Well, you got a job don't cha? So why waste your time?"

"Look ma, I'm gonna be gone tonight," he said as he got up to wash his dishes, "So don't worry about me comin' home, okay?"

"Where you gonna be? Eddie's?" her voice trembled.

"Yeah, Eddie's," he lied and felt horrible. He hated to lie to her.

It was bad enough he had to hide half the money he made to buy his bus tickets to Venice Beach.

He picked up his backpack and skateboard and bent over to kiss her on the cheek.

He knew he had a chance at winning the skateboard contest. Even if he didn't win, at this point he just felt good about getting out of Barstow…alone. Most of the time he felt lonely anyway. Boarding was an outlet for him to get away from the pain of being left by his father and having to deal with his mother.

Terrence had a shot at making something of himself; this was an opportunity he couldn't pass up.

Six
Mingmei Wong, Venice Beach, California

Mingmei Wong nervously paced around her tiny apartment waiting for her agent to call. She had just quit her job at the local sushi bar and needed money. She just couldn't stand having to clean raw fish for one more day. The slimy guts made her sick to her stomach.

She thought about wiring home for money, but knew she would be admitting failure. Something her proud Asian parents were waiting for. They were against her moving away from Texas to California to become an actress to begin with; especially since she had gotten a college scholarship when she graduated from high school two years earlier. They would never let her forget it. It was a huge disappointment for her family.

But Mingmei didn't want to become an accountant like her father, and she certainly didn't want to get married to her high school sweetheart to appease her mother. She wanted to follow her dream, and moving to California to become an actress was it.

She had worked hard to lose her Texan accent and land some acting roles. But that was between waitressing,

22

working at a dry cleaner, secretarial work, gardening, walking dogs and any other kind of temporary job she could find to support herself.

Now Mingmei was completely broke. She couldn't wait any longer. She picked up the phone and punched in her agent's number.

"Can I please speak with Mr. Handler?" she asked in a low tone, disguising her voice.

"Hi, May, let me see if he'll take your call," said the receptionist as the phone went silent.

Darn! Mingmei thought to herself, she had used that voice too many times!

"Mingmei! May, May, May. Helllloooo Mingmei, what can I do for you?" rasped her shifty-voiced agent, raw and smelly from too many cheap cigars.

"Listen, you still need some work on those voiceovers, but I think I can get you on that new soap *Hearts Connecting*. Auditions next Friday…just give me…"

"No!" snapped Mingmei holding back her tears as her voice quivered, "You promised me a real part. I want the show that I read for this week! I had three call backs for it and I need a job. You said I had the part!"

"Listen Ming…Hon, I know it's tough out here. You're a good kid. Competition is fierce. Maybe acting's not your thing. Anyway, look, I got a call today for a good-looking girl to pass out key chains for a shoe company. It's for one of the big sponsors at some kinda boarding energy drink competition thing. You know they surf, skate, whatever. It's put on by a soda company. You're a skater, right? Weren't you the one who skated in a commercial? Or you told me it's your hobby or somethin' like that. Anyway you don't even have to skate. All you have to do is stand there and look like your pretty little self. You'll be outside, get some fresh air, relax, give ya time to think…" The words were spewing out of her fast-talking agent's mouth when she interrupted.

"The only thing I want to think about are my lines for that part you promised me!"

"Listen, Ming, this gig pays 200 bucks for one day at the beach. How could you turn this down?"

There was silence until Mingmei gritted her teeth and replied, "What time and where?"

She hung up the phone, knowing in her heart there were plenty of other things she should be doing at 19 years old. Handing out free key chains to a bunch of surfer skateboard bums wasn't one of them. She also knew they would make more money winning a silly competition than she had made in the last two years.

She thought about all the skateboarding she had done. Her idiot agent hadn't even remembered that she had been the principal character in two commercials boarding!

It was something she had gotten into when she first moved to Los Angeles. Mingmei decided to try it when she found an old skateboard someone left behind in her apartment. She did it to keep in shape and fell in love with it. She was a natural and could board with some of the best of them at any of the parks. She was an excellent surfer, too.

Mingmei hit redial. The receptionist didn't want to put the agent back on the phone, but Mingmei begged and pleaded.

"Just a quick question…I promise," said Mingmei urgently.

"Yeah, I'm waiting," rasped her agent.

"Is it a co-ed competition?" Mingmei asked.

"Nope. All boys 16-18 years old," he retorted, "be there by 1pm sharp. Look hot. Ciao!"

Click.

The phone went dead. Mingmei walked into her kitchen and pulled a pair of scissors out of a drawer. She went to her bathroom, looked in the mirror and quickly began to cut off her hair.

Seven
1758 England

The villagers watched as the small black carriage passed through Twickenshire. It was lead by three noblemen heading toward the castle.

For years laborers had worked on the castle day and night, while the villagers watched the finest materials go by. During the last several months hundreds of horse-drawn carts filled with the best furniture and decorations from around the world made their way to the castle.

All the villagers knew about the owner – Duke Gregario Cloon de Sade – was that he had built the magnificent castle for his wife, the Duchess, after she gave birth to twin sons. Now that the boys were 10 years old, the castle was finally finished.

This weekend, all the townspeople were invited to the castle grounds for a massive festival in celebration of the arrival of the wealthy Cloon de Sade family. They dressed in their finest garments, prepared their best dishes and brought gifts to honor the twin boys.

Twickenshire was already a successful town on the outskirts of London. It was filled with many businessmen, doctors, lawyers, noblemen and diplomats. However, it was rumored that the Duke could turn their town into an even bigger mecca of business and wealth.

The celebration was an elaborate affair. It covered the inside of the spectacular castle, as well as the breathtaking grounds of lush gardens and beautiful flowering trees. The castle towered above as it sat overlooking a cliff with sparkling blue water to one side and dense forest on the other.

There were countless tables overflowing with delicious food. People were dancing and laughing as musicians and jesters entertained. It was the most fantastic event, and everyone was abuzz waiting to meet the exceptional family.

Trumpets began to sound as the Duke, Duchess and their two twin boys approached the outdoor stage. The Duke was a short thin man with a heavy black mustache and long black wavy hair. His wife was breathtakingly beautiful with ivory skin, fine features and thick curly red hair. She was dressed exquisitely in a stunning gown. The handsome twin boys Addison and Alistair were dressed identically in the finest apparel and seemed like playful, polite children.

But within seconds of the Duke's welcoming remarks, one of the twin boys had sprung from his seat and began to punch the other in the head! The Duchess cried out as she attempted to stop them. The boys continued to fight;

suddenly they jumped off the stage as one of them began to chase the other through the massive crowd of guests!

The Duke made light of the situation as he continued to thank everyone for coming. But the boys were terrors! They threw food, bumped into people and knocked things over! The Duke and Duchess finally went after them with their servants as they tried to get the boys under control. The Duchess emphatically apologized to the guests for the twins' behavior.

Once they had the boys restrained, she again made excuses for them as they dragged them back toward the castle kicking and screaming. She continued to explain that the castle was new to them and that everything had been a bit overwhelming for the twins. It was clear to everyone that she was completely embarrassed, while the Duke seemed barely fazed.

Eight
Harlo's Dream

Harlo worked at the restaurant late into the evening. When he got home he skated until the wee hours of the morning by the single hanging light bulb above the old garage.

He barely slept, and by six in the morning he was back at the quaint crab shack helping his dad. Four hours later, he was done.

"Okay, I finished painting the back door and cleaned out the ice machine. I put all the clean plates away and I polished the hostess stand, refilled the salt, pepper and bay seasoning and mopped the floor, restocked the newspaper for the tables and screwed all the new mallets together! Can I go now?" Harlo choked, he had told his father what he had done at such rapid speed he could barely catch his breath.

"Whoa…slow down…you did all that this morning?" His father asked in amazement.

Breathing deeply, Harlo quickly nodded.

"Yeah, then go! Go win!" laughed his father.

"Sweeeet!" yelled Harlo, as he grabbed his skateboard and took off out the door.

"I hope he wins this thing. It's all he thinks about!" said Harlo's dad to his mother.

"Yeah, me too, I would hate to see him disappointed about losing another contest."

Harlo quickly strapped on his helmet and jumped on his skateboard. He stooped and ducked as he gained maximum speed heading down the sidewalk along the beach toward the boardwalk. He knew in his heart that if he didn't win this competition, he would spend the rest of his life working at King's Crab Shack. Not that it was such a bad place; most people would love to have that kind of opportunity. But Harlo dreamed of seeing the world.

He could hear the echo of the speaker and the loud sounds coming from just behind the boardwalk where the contest was taking place. He strained to hear what the announcer was saying, but his wheels were grinding so fast that it was just hollow sounds.

He ollied up the sidewalk, rode past the old buildings and turned the corner. He breathed a sigh of relief to see that the contest hadn't started. He hopped off his board, caught it, and ran to the registration booth to sign up. He just made it!

He quickly slapped his large sticky patch with his competition number on his t-shirt, filled in the paperwork on the clipboard and attached his signed permission slip.

He was walking to the holding area when he heard someone shout his name.

"King! Kiinnngg!"

"Jake! Dominic, Ben! How's it going?" asked Harlo turning toward his friends. He walked up to them and happily gave them a high-five then plopped down on a bench.

"I wouldn't relax if I were you," said Ben.

"Oh, no? Why not?" asked Harlo, while putting on his knee and elbow pads and helmet.

"Well for starters, there are people here from like everywhere, dude! Rehoboth Beach, Salisbury, Annapolis…you name it! Some people even came in from Baltimore & D.C.! It's like totally the comp to enter!" said Jake excitedly.

"Yeah, I'm just glad I made it," sighed Harlo.

The contest began. It started with the street competition. There were tons of straight and curving rails and steps set up, benches and ramps with coping and gaps. Then there was the vert.

Harlo was surprised at how quickly the judges eliminated people – one after another. He began to wonder if his being last in the contest would affect the judging. He knew this was the biggest challenge he had ever entered; the prize package, plus the worldwide tour was huge. But what

Harlo hadn't anticipated was how tough the judges were going to be.

If a competitor was the least bit sketchy, they were out!

Some of the skaters splat to the concrete within seconds of starting. But Harlo was amazed by the tricks cranked out by some really great boarders. They were doing 360s, frontside heel flips and backside noseslides and tricks he had never ever seen before! He was psyched. He knew he would have to pull out his best uninhibited tricks for this contest.

"Harlo King!" called one of the Sisu Soda staff. It was finally his turn. He took his place on the platform, took a deep breath and listened for the MC to announce his name. When he did, Harlo immediately began with an ollie heel flip varial, then a hard flip to manual on the box 180 out to nose manual. Harlo held the manual for almost a full lap around the park! He then kicked and headed for the small kinked rail and pulled a K-grind. With time running out he went for some old-school and ollied up a retaining wall to a Casper half-impossible out.

The crowd went nuts! He finished off with a huge boneless into a small transition straight to a no comply to manual and made the full lap this time. As sweat poured off him, he jumped off his board and with a quick kick, his board shot up into his right hand, he caught it and took a bow.

He moved to the other side, thrilled he hadn't been eliminated. Now came the hard part. The vert was the next round.

The second he heard his name, Harlo dropped in with a huge front side air to gain momentum, then pumped the transition as hard as he could and threw a McTwist right off the bat. Again he wowed the crowd! Next, Harlo threw a Benihana, followed by an amazing Caballerial. *'No way!'* he thought to himself, *'I can't believe I stuck that!'* Changing it up a bit, Harlo pulled a Hurricane, one of his favorites. That's a 180 to backwards feeble grind 270 out! Harlo was feeling good as he finished off with a Smith Grind that spanned the length of the vert and an Egg plant on the other side. Finally coming back, he ollied up onto the deck and threw his hands up.

He heard his name and thought for sure he was being eliminated…

"Harlo King – Ocean City, Maryland!" roared the MC into the microphone.

He spun and ollie ooped to the top. He couldn't believe he had made it! While catching his breath, it seemed like an eternity as the judges compared notes. Harlo stood frozen as he watched a judge move to the MC. He began to announce the two runners up. The first name, then the second, and then…"The grand prize winner in the Sisu Soda 'Thrash Energy Drink Contest'-- Harlo King of Ocean City, Maryland!"

Harlo was in shock! This time he had won!

Nine
Donell's Lie

"Take LaKeesha with you today," said Donell's mother.

"Uh, not today mom. I c...can't," Donell stuttered.

"What do you mean, you c...can't? I have to go to work and your dad is working overtime at the plant. Your brother has had plans for weeks to help at the library. You can certainly take your sister with you. She is not going to interrupt your basketball game," his mother hollered.

"Okay, alright. I will..." answered Donell, "*try to talk my brother into taking her with him*," He continued quietly under his breath as his mother left the room.

Donell watched her leave the house then quickly went downstairs and begged and pleaded with his brother to take his sister with him. He was forced to tell him that he wasn't really going to play basketball, that he was really entering a skateboard competition.

"Are you nuts? You'll be grounded forever if dad finds out you've been lyin' about basketball! Not only that, but skateboardin?! Here come 'mere, lemme check to see if you have a fever!" said his brother acting like he was going to check Donell's head.

"Get outta here! I don't have no fever, fool!" snapped Donell pushing his brother's hand away, "I know I can win this thing and the prize is huge! I'll have a sponsor and it'll pay for half my college! C'mon...I'll give you my car for a week!"

"You don't have a car!"

"I mean when I get one."

"Two weeks of your allowance," argued his brother.

"No way!" yelled Donell.

"Hmmm...Must not be so sure you're gonna win that huge prize, huh?"

"Alright, two weeks' allowance, but you can forget about ever using my car...when I get one," Donell snapped as he pulled out his wallet and peeled off two five dollar bills. He tossed them at his brother and stormed out of the room.

"Car...you must've bumped your head skateboardin'...skateboardin! Hmmmph!" laughed his brother.

After giving his brother two weeks of his hard-earned allowance, it made him question his skating ability as he ripped down the alley to meet Andre and Keyshawn. Andre had talked his brother into driving them to the event at the state fairgrounds.

When they arrived at the grounds, they quickly found their way in to register. A band was playing on one

36

side of the huge vert ramp. Shoe, magazine, clothing, sporting goods, and all sorts of other companies had booths set up everywhere with people passing out free stuff.

Sisu Soda's tent was the biggest of all, and they were giving away free cans of their new energy drink – Thrash.

They each grabbed one of the tall, slender silver cans with neon purple stripes, chugged it down and quickly made their way to sign in. They took their numbers and found their places on the bench while filling in their applications. Donell felt sick inside as he attached the forged note.

The contest began right on time. Donell, Andre, and Keyshawn sat watching the first few competitors. They weren't at all impressed. One by one the skateboarders tumbled, fell, wobbled and were sketchy as they were disqualified.

They were from all walks of life, from the suburbs to small town teams. Some were dressed like clones. Others, so ridiculous they made the audience laugh.

As Donell sat watching, he grew serious when he began to think about what would happen if he really won. *How would he would ever convince his father to let him tour?*

Andre and Keyshawn began chatting about how they were going to put on such an excellent performance that Sisu Soda would have to take all of them on tour!

"Donell James, Donell James," said the MC.

"Knock 'em out!" said Andre excitedly.

Donell approached the stage while putting on his helmet. He instantly felt sick inside as he looked out at the crowd. It was one thing to skate with your friends, yet another to be staring at hundreds of strangers. He took his position at the top of the vert.

He knew he had to win, so he decided to go all out. Donell could skate better than anyone because of his ability to blend old school style with current technical tricks. Mounting his board with his tall slender physique he took off.

The crowd roared with excitement as he did a backside 540! His dreadlocks looked like they were spikes standing on end as he pumped the trany! One down, he thought as he made it up the vert. The crowd roared!

Donell finished his round and rejoined Andre and Keyshawn, who were now furious with him.

"What?" asked Donell.

"You dissed us, man!" snapped Keyshawn, just as the MC called Keyshawn's name.

"No look man…! I just couldn't do what we had planned!"

But it was too late. Keyshawn was so angry that he punched Donell in the arm – hard! It was enough to make the judges take note and immediately Keyshawn was disqualified.

"Man, it was the three of us and you let us down!" said Keyshawn as he went to leave.

"Your just trippin' cuz you lost your temper! Now lay off!" barked Andre.

Andre was up next, and he agreed with Donell that he had to give it his all. Andre made the cut. But the next round wasn't going to be so easy. This was a challenge for only the best. "Come on Donell, were gonna need to be at ease to make this."

Andre was right; the second half of the competition would consist of skating in a giant full pipe. They had to skate in three complete circles just to make it through the course.

There were only five skaters left. One after the other they fell off their boards, or were called out by the judges for other mistakes.

By the end of the first round through the loop-de-loop of the giant full pipe, Donell knew that he had won. Even though in his heart, he felt he had lost a precious friendship.

Ten
For a Friend

Pal had fallen off the skateboard for the last time! After practicing countless tricks at the skateboard park and in his driveway, he was sick of getting bruised. He picked himself up off the black asphalt. Pal decided the only boarding he would be doing was for pleasure. If his buddy Steven wanted someone to win that competition, he could enter it himself...

BEEP BEEP BEEP BEEP!!!!

The horn startled Pal out of his thoughts as Steven roared up the driveway in his tiny rusted-out convertible.

"Bro! You just about scared my shorts off!" yelled Pal.

"Sorry, dude. You ready?"

"I changed my mind," said Pal, scowling as he brushed dirt off himself, "Look, I totally ruined my new Hawaiian shirt!"

"You can't tell, besides you have others like that..."

"Are you saying all my Hawaiian shirts look the same?" snapped Pal.

"Look, bro, like I know why you are trying to argue with me! You can win this competition! You just have to pretend it's the waves, dude. Besides, you've already mastered some of the most difficult tricks! I saw you riding that skateboard yesterday like it was nobody's business. Now get in and let's go do some skate boardin'! It'll be fun! What have you got to lose?"

Pal took a deep breath as he turned and looked at his family's mansion.

"Goodbye easy life…" he whined, as he threw the skateboard into the back of the car and jumped in over the door.

Steven stared at Pal since he had never seen him jump like that.

"Pretty good for a fat boy, eh?" laughed Pal.

Steven burst out laughing as he shifted into gear. His car sputtered down the beach road.

At the competition, they greeted friends and strolled around the hugely decorated area. Brightly colored flags were waving in the breeze. Two giant inflatable cans designed like the Thrash Energy Drinks were at the entrance. Pretty girls were passing out promotional stuff as Pal stopped to flirt with them while Steven pulled him away.

There were sponsor tents everywhere. Music was blaring while people poured in to watch the competition. A huge vert ramp was glistening in the sun.

Even though the event was much bigger than they expected, Pal relaxed a bit. He liked the excitement and the

41

crowds. He decided he was doing this for fun; even though he could feel a twinge of competition welling up inside.

"You need to check in, my man!" said Steven excitedly. He had taken on the role of Pal's manager and Pal didn't mind.

"What if I don't win? You'll still have to let me pay you for managing me these last few days," exclaimed Pal.

"Bro, you'll win!" said Steven, as he handed him the application to fill out and attached the permission form from Pal's parents.

"C'mon, let's get up front!" said Steven.

They found a seat in the front row of the crowded competitor area.

"Excuse me. May I have your entry form?" A man in a purple Sisu Soda shirt asked Pal.

Pal handed him his application.

"And yours?" the man hurriedly asked Steven.

"Oh, I'm not entering," replied Steven.

"Then you'll have to wait in the audience bleachers," insisted the man.

"Well, see, I'm his manager and I…"

Just then the MC started the contest. The man shook his head and walked away.

Pal and Steven happily gave each other a thumbs-up, but their attitudes quickly changed as they watched the first few competitors.

"Ahhh, no way dude…I'm not…" began Pal.

But it was too late.

"Contestant number three, from Kapaa, Kauai, Hawaii - Freddy Palamau!" the MC announced.

"That's you bro! Go!" said Steven as he pushed a stunned Pal toward the gate, "Ride like you did this week at the skateboard park, bro! Pretend the wheels are like your waves! Ride like the waves!"

Pal got ready to ride while feeling out of place after seeing the other toned, muscular boarders. Then something happened, a small rumble came from the audience and he could hear Steven and others start chanting…" Freeeedddy! Freeedddy!"

The next thing he knew, more people were chanting! He did his first trick while the chant grew louder! He was totally enjoying the limelight!

Pal decided he would put his personality into it as he grinded down the twelve step rail.

His friend Steven was right! He could do this! His weeks of constant skating paid off. It was then and there that Pal decided a short, chubby boy from Kauai could do anything he set his mind to! He was on fire!

He came to a screeching halt while the crowd cheered. Pal enjoyed the spotlight, as much as the spotlight loved him. He gave it his all and ended up winning the grand prize! For Pal, even though this wasn't the life that he had planned, the thought thrilled him!

Eleven
Two Can Win

The bus door opened and a rush of cold air hit Terrence in the face. He was relieved as he climbed in. The mix of emotions he had felt from nervousness to sadness, anger to apprehension seemed to drift away. He was on his way to Venice Beach and nothing could stop him now.

He grabbed a seat with an elderly man who was snoring. He put his headphones on and sat back to relax as the bus began rolling through the beautiful California terrain.

Suddenly, the bus stopped with a jolt. Terrence immediately woke up thinking that something had gone wrong, until he realized that he, too, had dozed off.

"Venice Beach, California. Please make sure to gather your belongings and depart through the front exit," said the bus driver.

Terrence quickly gathered his stuff. Once outside the bus, he looked around and noticed that sunny Los Angeles seemed awfully gray and cloudy. He got out his street map and within seconds was on his board flying toward the contest location.

He could see the brightly colored displays as he rounded the street corner toward the center of the park near the competition on the beach.

Mingmei stopped and pulled her hat down, then zipped her baggy jacket all the way up. She walked through the gates and picked up an application. She filled it out, relieved that it didn't say anything about being male, and there was no actual age limit on it – only in the advertisements. She turned around to hand in her application when someone bumped into her. It sent the clipboard flying out of her hand!

"Oh, sorry dude! Really sorry! My bad…" said Terrence as he picked up the papers and clipboard.

"No, really, it's okay…" said a soft voice, "I mean no problem, dude!" came a much deeper tone.

Terrence warily handed the clipboard over to what he thought was a strange guy and got in line to sign up.

He watched as the person in the hat nervously turned in his papers with his head down then scurried away. Terrence realized that what he had heard about the Los Angeles area was true; there were lots of wild and crazy people.

He signed in, took a spot in the competitor zone, and waited with at least a hundred other hopefuls. He tried not to think about the competition as he visualized what he would do on his board.

46

Next the MC announced – Ming Wong. It was the little Asian kid that Terrence had bumped into. He watched as the strange kid took his place, then began. He couldn't believe his eyes, this guy was phenomenal!

He dropped in and pumped the transition hard straight into a front side air for some umph! Then he blasted back down and up the other side pulling a huge fakie mute 360. Someone from the crowd yelled, "Go grabless!" So he did! He pumped again and this time pulled the more difficult Caballero, pumped the trany one more time then up the other side into a massive Madonna! The way he was skating was something Terrence had never seen before!

The oddest thing was that this kid had to be roasting! He was still wearing his hat, jacket and long pants in the 90-degree temperatures. Terrence knew if he was going to beat this kid, he was going to have to work really hard. But that was something he was used to doing.

Terrence pushed his long, wavy blond hair back and strapped on his helmet. He decided to check his king-pin to make sure it was tight, and just in time, his name was called! He took his place, then dropped in on the vert ramp. Terrence pumped hard as he went right into a huge Christ Air. He was doing the best skateboarding he had ever done! He knew he had to be in the finals when he finished with a 720!

Suddenly the overcast sky split apart; massive clouds poured heavy rain on the entire event!

The contest would have to stop until the rain subsided. It was the longest half hour of his life. When the skies finally cleared, the Sisu Soda people quickly came out to dry off the huge ramp.

During the second round the competition was even more fierce. The Wong kid did some extraordinary tricks, including some unbelievable anti-caspers. It was almost like the kid could fly!

Terrence thought about how he was just as good as the strange hat-wearing kid, and how this was his only way out of Barstow. He slammed his front trucks down and focused on his tricks.

By the end of the second round, Terrence was exhausted. He had pulled out some of his best stuff and the judges seemed to be taking an extra long time deciding the winner. Then came the announcement…

"In order to make a fair and competent choice, the judges have a split decision. Based on Sisu Soda's Thrash Energy Drink Contest, they have decided to add an additional grand prize winner!" shouted the excited MC.

Two winners! That meant two grand prize winners! Terrence's mind raced, there was only supposed to be one! He eyed the Wong kid who was two rows in front of him.

"Our two, yes two, grand prize winners of the Sisu Soda and Thrash Energy Drink, Challenge Yourself Because You'll Be Challenged competition are Ming Wong of Venice Beach, California, and Terrence Zevon of Barstow, California!"

"Yes! Yes!" screamed Terrence as he jumped up and down! People rushed over to congratulate him! Terrence turned around to shake hands with the Ming Wong kid, but he had already left.

Twelve
The Evil Duke

Duke Cloon de Sade's throat tightened as he pounded his fist on the table, "Barnard Tibley may I inform you that this is a mere pittance of what you owe me!"

Mr. Tibley wiped the sweat from his brow and nodded as he stared at his desk in his small dark storefront. The curtains were still drawn with the engraved closed sign on the door. He trembled as he thought about what the evil Duke would do to him.

"What, pray tell, do you intend to do about it?" the Duke questioned evilly.

"You have bled me dry! I am out of money! You promised me you would…"

"SILENCE!" bellowed the Duke as he moved to peek out of the small window in the heavy wood door as Mr. Tibley began to sob.

The Duke moved swiftly back to the elderly man and grabbed him by the ruffled white ties on the front of his sweat drenched shirt and yanked him to his feet. He began to choke Tibley. Tibley wrestled to free himself, but could no longer breathe. When he almost passed out, the Duke dropped him to the floor coughing and gasping for air.

"You shouldn't be in business if you don't know what you're doing!" sneered the Duke as he kicked Tibley in the stomach. He then grabbed the small bag of money from the table, eyed a silver pipe and mug, stuck them in his pocket and left.

The Tibley family had once been one of the wealthiest in the county, and now they were almost broke thanks to the despicable dealings of the Duke Cloon de Sade. Mr. Tibley could never figure it out. It seemed to happen almost overnight; ever since they began attending the Cloon de Sade's parties. Somehow the Duke had figured out everything about Tibley's earnings and business – enough to make it look like his deals were shady, and blackmail him.

The 15-year-old twins were waiting outside on their horses for their father.

"Looks like a bag of money!" said Addison loudly.

"Quiet your voice," snapped the Duke looking around suspiciously.

"Father, you promised me a new stallion…" said Alistair as he reached down and grabbed the bag of money from his father's hand.

"Give me that!" yelled the Duke as people began to stop and stare.

"No, this time father promised me his earnings!" yelled Addison as he jumped down off of his horse and yanked his brother off of his. Within seconds the 15-year-old twins were rolling on the ground fighting for the bag of money. They punched and hit each other until the bag ripped open and money spilled out all over the ground.

The crowd of people that had now formed, immediately dove for the coins, before long a small riot had broke out! The bloodied twins stood up to watch their father riding away from the commotion, furious.

When the twins arrived back at the castle the Duchess was enraged to see her son's beaten and battered.

"What did you do to the boys?" she demanded as the Duke sat in his library counting money.

"Nothing! They did it to themselves!" he barked without looking up.

"Stop taunting them with your devious schemes! You're ruining these boys! They don't know what love is, only money. Please, I beg you to stop before it's too late!" the Duchess pleaded, but the Duke continued to ignore her.

Thirteen
King of the Contest

Harlo was excited beyond belief! To add to his excitement even more, his family had surprised him by showing up! His mother and father were jumping up and down in the bleachers. As much as they wanted Harlo to follow in the family business, they were thrilled to see him realize his dream.

Harlo was given a cool metal trophy that was modeled after the Thrash Energy Drink can on a skateboard, and a giant-sized check for $200,000, plus a $50,000 scholarship! Harlo's hands were shaking as he took the prizes.

He was then escorted to the courtesy tent to meet with the sponsors. He was told that his plane tickets would arrive in two weeks; then he would be required to leave for the world tour. He was given his passport instructions and departure information.

Harlo would be challenged in other board events throughout the tour. The sponsors gave him a backpack filled with free items; he couldn't believe this was happening!

"We are so proud of you!" he heard his mother crying behind him.

"Way to go, son!" said his dad.

"Can I have your room?" asked his brother.

Later that night, Harlo's parents held a party at the crab shack with family and friends. It was the best night of his life!

Yet, he couldn't wait until later in the evening when he could get back to his laptop. He desperately wanted to get online to tell his new friend GT that he won the contest. He also wanted to tell him that the first stop on the tour would be London, England.

Fourteen
For the Family

Donell received the grand prize and was escorted to the tent and given tour instructions. They took his measurements for the Sisu Soda apparel he would have to wear – right down to his fingers. As they left the tent, Andre told everyone they passed by that Donell was the world's best skateboarder!

It was bittersweet for Donell, since his friend Keyshawn had left angry.

"Forgetta 'bout him! He's just mad cuz he didn't win," said Andre.

Donell knew that Andre was right, but he also knew he was in for a bigger challenge telling his father the news.

"Donell Anthony James, is that you?" his mother yelled from the kitchen.

"Yeah it's me," he replied, closing the barred door to the old brick home.

"You're late for dinner!" hollered his mother, "And just explain to me as to why you deliberately disobeyed me? Why didn't you take your sister with you to the library like I told you to?!"

55

Donell knew he was in trouble, but didn't expect his mother to be this mad. Then it hit him – his brother had spilled the beans! Donell swallowed and slowly walked into the kitchen.

"DONELL'S IN TROUBLE...DONELL'S IN TROUBLE!!!" chanted all of his brothers and sisters in unison.

"Be silent!" his father yelled as he pounded his fist on the table.

Everyone at the dinner table froze, nobody moved.

Donell knew by the look on his father's face he was furious!

"Dad, let me explain," said Donell as he sat down at the table. His father continued eating in silence.

"Please, you have to hear me out..."

"You have thrown away my trust in you, Donell," said his father while jabbing at his pork chop.

"But I did it for you!" Donell pleaded.

"For me?! For me! You lied and snuck around behind my back saying you were playin' basketball! All the while you were out doin' some ridiculous sport like skateboardin'! How in the heck did you do that for me?"

"I won the contest!" said Donell.

"Well, is that a fact? And just what do you expect to do with winning a silly skateboarding contest? What did you win? A t-shirt? Some stickers? Just how the heck is that going to put you through college?"

"No, Dad, I won this…it'll pay for my first year of college and a lot more!"

Donell slowly pulled the check for $200,000 plus the scholarship papers out of his pocket.

His father put on his glasses and read the paper while his mother leaned back in her chair trying to see over his shoulder. When she saw the amount of the check she gasped and almost fell backwards off her chair!

His dad cleared his throat as he stared at the papers. His mother began to wipe tears from her eyes.

"Uh-huh, this says you have to go on tour. Just who the heck is gonna pay for that? Huh? That's where all this dang money will go!"

"No, Dad, that's for us and our family. They pay for the tour," said Donell, "plus I get tons of free gear like this…" Donell jumped up and ran to get the backpack they had given him. "Plus, this will give me the opportunity to try out for things like the World Cup!"

Donell began to pass out the contents of his backpack to his excited brothers and sisters.

"My, my! I happen to know that Sisu Soda is one big company! They have offices right here in Michigan. I did hear about this contest thing. But had no idea my boy Donell

57

was even thinking about entering," said his mother talking rapidly while trying hard to contain her excitement.

Donell held his breath, waiting.

After several seconds his father ordered him to his room.

The kitchen was still as Donell got up and left.

Two hours passed, but it seemed like forever, when Donell finally heard his father call him. He flew out of his room and down the stairs.

"Your mama and I are extremely disappointed that you didn't have the sense to discuss this with us," said his father, "and the fact that you must've signed my name to enter. Didn't you?"

Donell clenched his hands together in fear as he stared at the floor and nodded.

"But since your heart was in the right place, you can go on that Thrash whatever tour."

Donell sat upright looking at his father.

"But only because it is the opportunity of a lifetime. But you will, and I mean *will* have to earn my trust in you again, son! If you ever…"

Donell was so excited that he jumped up and ran over to hug his father while his mother began screaming and jumping up and down.

Donell had not only achieved his dreams, but helped his parents fulfill theirs.

Fifteen
New Beginning

Pal was thrilled that he had won the competition. Even more thrilled when they handed him the huge check.

"Wow wee wow wow!" said Steven, looking over Pal's shoulder.

"No kidding! You know part of this is yours. And by the way, Mr. Manager…What shall I call you?" asked Pal happily as they headed to Steven's convertible.

"I think…I like what you always call me – Bro," answered Steven with a wide grin.

"Well then, let's go break this crazy news to my parents, *bro*," said Pal.

"Really, dude? I thought you already told them," asked Steven concerned.

"Oh yeah, I told them I was entering alright, and my dad signed the papers through his tears."

"Through his tears?   Before you said he had laughed about it," questioned Steven.

"He did. He laughed so hard he was crying," chuckled Pal, "and I don't blame him. Imagine me, Freddy 'Pal' Palamau, a skateboarding champion? Kind of ridiculous."

"It's cuz of all that boarding you do, man. I mean boarding is boarding, plus you really practiced day and night."

"Yeah, no doubt, plus what you taught me!" laughed Pal pointing at his bruises.

When they got to the hotel office, Pal's parents didn't believe he won, until Pal showed them the award and giant check. They were shocked as they told him how happy they were for him, and glad that he would get to see the world.

"And if you decide that you want to come back and run the business after the tour, we're here," said Pal's father.

Pal and Steven left to share the news with their friends.

The next evening the Palamau family treated everyone to a giant Luau at their hotel. It was an exciting night, even the local news showed up to interview Pal.

Pal loved being on camera, hamming it up; but remembered to pull his best friend into the interview as his manager. Steven nervously nodded while Pal did the talking.

Later that evening when the excitement subsided, Pal watched as Mr. Palamau handed Steven the keys to a small unused office in the hotel. He said it was a place for him to start his 'manager' business. But, in exchange he would have to leave the hamburger stand and work for him at the hotel part time.

"Yes!" shouted Steven and they celebrated their new careers.

Sixteen
Problems

When Terrence entered the Sisu Soda tent he could hear the Ming kid arguing about giving his measurements. He said that he wasn't feeling well, and he would email his sizes to them later.

They finally agreed, but it was apparent they thought he was strange, too. Ming finished the paperwork, and they handed him a backpack full of stuff as he headed out of the tent – fast.

Next it was Terrence's turn; he also had a major problem. They insisted that they needed to deliver his tickets to his home. Terrence explained that he would be staying in Los Angeles until the tour started. When they wanted the hotel address, he had nothing to give them.

They moved to the back of the tent to discuss the problem; Terrence could hear one of the female managers say, "Only in L.A.!"

After quite a bit of discussion, they agreed to send his tour papers and plane tickets to the hotel where they would be staying on the start date of the tour. But it was up to him to contact them with his passport information.

Because the Sisu Soda people would have to help make arrangements to get the passport rushed through.

Relieved, Terrence awkwardly finished the business end of things, but he suddenly felt alone. It was strange being in a big city by himself. He knew he would have to open a bank account before he could afford a hotel to stay in for the next couple of weeks. He looked around the vast park, deciding that the first thing he had to do was call his mother and tell her about the competition. When he thought about the fact that he had won, he couldn't help but feel excited.

He deposited change into the only pay phone he could find. It rang seven times before his mother finally picked up.

"Yeah…" she answered in a sleepy voice.

"Ma, it's me, are you sleeping again? Never mind, I called to tell you that I won't be coming home," He said sadly.

"I know you are at Eddie…that Eddie kid's whatever's name," she mumbled.

"No. No, I'm not at Eddie's. I'm in Los Angeles," stated Terrence firmly.

"Where? Why? Why are you so far away?" his mother whined into the phone.

The conversation continued, as he explained that he felt his leaving would force her to take care of herself and get herself together.

While she ranted and raved Terrence held the phone out away from his ear.

"I won't be coming back, Ma," he said solemnly into the receiver when she finally calmed down. Once again, Terrence was acting like he was the parent. He told her he would call her from the tour -- that if she would clean up, get a job, and take care of herself, he would send her money to help her out. She promised she would. Terrence hoped she meant it this time.

Seventeen
The Role of a Lifetime

Sitting on a park bench, Mingmei finally cooled down after taking off her hat, and hot sweaty jacket and rolling up her pant legs. Her hair was soaked with sweat. As she combed it back with her fingers she noticed the other kid who won the competition across the park. From where she sat he couldn't see her, and without her hat and coat on, and with her huge sunglasses she knew he wouldn't recognize her.

To her it looked like he was arguing with someone on a pay phone. She wondered why he didn't have a cell phone. She thought about how she always considered boarders as rebels, but he seemed different to her. He seemed smart and kind.

Her mind quickly went back to thinking about how thrilled she was that she had won the money! Now she could pay her overdue bills.

She wasn't quite sure what to do about the fact that she had to go on tour with the long-haired blond boy, and a bunch of other males. She wondered if she could actually pull it off...pretending to be a boy! It was like something out of a movie, only the men and women who dress up in movies as the opposite sex usually didn't have to skateboard! Dressing up like a boy for a year would be tough; it would be a true test of her acting skills.

She pulled out her cell phone to check her messages. She was startled when she heard her agent's raspy voice screaming at her, "That's it Ming, you coulda made two hundred bucks just to show up and hand out key chains today! But noooo…you are ungrateful! I am dropping you as a client today! Now go see how many acting jobs you can get!"

At first Ming laughed to herself, but then decided that was it. Hearing her mean agent's voice, she knew she'd have to take on the challenge of the tour. If she could pull off this stunt, she would be able to get any agent in town. Mingmei picked up her sweaty hat and jacket and headed back to her tiny apartment down the street, excited about her new role!

Eighteen
Ghost Hunters No More

Emily sat bleary-eyed at her computer in her flat above the pub. Derek, the pub owner had been kind enough to rent her the small, quaint apartment for a deal.

It had hardwood floors and stucco walls; Emily made it homey with her decorating skills. It was the perfect place for her to write her book and do research on the Castle Cloon de Sade.

It was two o' clock in the morning and she was exhausted. After shutting down her laptop, she climbed into bed and turned off her lamp.

Suddenly there was a pounding on the door downstairs! Emily was so frightened it felt like her heart stopped! She quickly put on her robe and forced open the window and shutters and peered down through the darkness.

Downstairs, at the entrance to the pub, she could see flashing lights and the police.

"I'll be right down!" she yelled.

Once downstairs, she unlocked the eight bolts on the pub door. Derek always laughed about the locks calling them the poltergeist protectors.

The officer tipped his hat and excused himself for bothering her at such a late hour. "Have you ever seen these before, miss?" He asked, as he held up a bloody satchel and jacket.

Emily immediately recognized them. They were the belongings of the men she had waited on earlier in the evening! The ghost hunters!

Emily nodded as she shuddered, "Are they dead?"

"No, miss, we just wondered if anyone in these parts had seen them before. They were found beaten and screaming for help while crawling down Brogden Street. They are at the hospital in shock."

Emily gave details on what she knew about the ghost hunters; what they told her of their plans. The police officer shook his head and said he would need to take her down to the hospital to identify them. She agreed and quickly phoned Derek.

As Emily closed the old door to the pub she locked every bolt on it, terrified that she would have to venture out on such a dreadful night.

Nineteen
Meeting in LA

LAX was much bigger than Harlo imagined. He walked toward baggage claim gripping his laptop tightly under his arm. He was nervous being on a trip by himself for the first time as he followed the airport escort.

Once they reached the baggage claim, Harlo waited next to the turnstile. The escort met with a neatly dressed man in a captain's hat who was holding up a 'Sisu Soda' sign.

Standing next to him was a short chubby guy in a loud Hawaiian print shirt and a tall thin black guy with dread locks.

Harlo turned back around almost missing his bag as he grabbed it. The escort came back and instructed him to join them and wished him good luck. Harlo ambled toward the group.

"Harlo King from Ocean City, Maryland," he introduced himself.

Harlo was instantly relieved to join his fellow boarders and now was looking forward to the journey. Plus, he had his Internet buddy, GT, with him. He always seemed to be available no matter what time of day or night, to instant message about the paranormal.

"Hello and welcome," said the chauffeur reaching for Harlo's bags, as Harlo gripped his computer tighter.

"Aloha, Freddy Palamau from the beautiful island of Kauai, Hawaii, but you can call me Pal," said Pal happily as he reached out to shake Harlo's hand. Harlo shook his hand, and then turned to the tall black man.

"Yeah, Donell James from magnificent city of Detroit and you can call me Donell," He said smirking.

"Well then, I believe we are all here," said the chauffeur. "I am to drive you to your hotel and make sure you're checked in. Your tour manager and guide, Mr. Ira Golden, has been detained. Therefore, he will meet you at the hotel."

"Detained? Must be an important man," shrugged Donell.

"Not as important as we are now!" joked Pal, acting like he was skateboarding. They laughed as the tension dissolved away.

Once outside the airport doors, there was an enormous black stretch limousine waiting. The chauffeur opened the doors for them as their mouths dropped open.

"Oh yeah, now your talkin' to me," said Donell.

"Uh-huh and loudly!" smiled Pal.

70

"Wow...like WOW!" said Harlo as he jumped into the back of the limousine.

The limo sped away from the airport as Pal opened the sunroof and they popped their heads out. They cracked jokes and laughed while sharing bits of information about themselves. They played with every gadget in the car – as they enjoyed Thrash Energy drinks in fancy glass goblets.

When the limousine pulled up to the front of the hotel they were shocked. It was one of the most famous and luxurious hotels in the world. It was a beautiful pink colored building with a distinct tiled roof. The grounds were exquisite with palm trees and exotic flowers everywhere.

"Man, these people spare no expense!" said Donell.

They looked in awe as they followed the chauffeur into the perfectly manicured hotel. The inside was as magnificent as the outside; huge chandeliers and stately columns were everywhere and beautiful furniture graced the lobby.

The chauffeur met with the concierge, checked them in and handed out their keys. They were guided to their rooms and instructed that their luggage would be delivered shortly. The concierge gave them strict instructions that they were to report downstairs promptly at 6:00 p.m.

Harlo was so stunned by the elegance of his room that he had to share it with his new boarding buddies. He knocked on the connecting door to Pal's room.

71

"Do you believe this, man? It's just gnarly!" Harlo exclaimed, as Pal opened the door.

"No joke, bro! Like my parents don't even stay in places like this and they have money! Hey! Let's see what our Detroit brother is up to."

"They left Pal's room and knocked on Donell's door across the hall, but he didn't bother to answer.

"I don't think he's too friendly," said Harlo.

"Ahhhh, he'll come around. He's a fellow boarder," said Pal.

They went back to Pal's room and stood on the huge balcony overlooking the beautiful pool area. It was filled with slim tan people sunbathing and relaxing. They chatted about the craziness of winning the competition and what their strongest boarding skill was. They compared their free stuff, including all the shoes and hats they had gotten from sponsors.

They talked about the upcoming events and their excitement about heading to London, England. They also talked about the second segment of the tour – they were glad that it was surfing. Since they had both grown up in ocean towns, it would be the easiest for both of them.

"Dude…it's five to six. We better get downstairs and meet our tour manager!" said Harlo eagerly.

"Yeah, like I bet he's totally cool!" said Pal.

They had no idea what they were in for.

Twenty
Ira Golden and Cheese

At 6:00 p.m. Pal, Harlo and Donell walked into the fantastic lobby. Their heads were constantly turning as celebrities and wild looking people strutted by them.

They sat down where two other people who looked like boarders were sitting; an Asian fellow and a blond surfer-looking guy.

"Are you the other Thrash contest winners?" Pal asked.

Ming slowly nodded, keeping her hat pulled down below her eyes. Ming and Terrence had been there fifteen minutes earlier, but hadn't said two words to each other. Even though Terrence had tried to talk to Ming, she would either nod or not answer.

"Yeah, hey! My name is Terrence Zevon. Barstow, California." Terrence said as he stood up to shake hands with everyone. He was relieved to see that there were some friendlier guys on the tour.

"Hello, I'm Freddy 'Pal' Palamau from beautiful Kauai, Hawaii, call me Pal."

"I'm Harlo and I'm from O.C. Maryland and happy to be here!"

"Donell James, Detroit, yeah I said Detroit, and people *do* actually live there."

"I'm Ming…*cough, cough*, Wong from Venice…*cough*…Beach," Ming was the only one who didn't fit in. She coughed her way through her introduction, while nervously working on her deep voice. She had practiced a lower tone for the last few days, but was still skeptical about it.

She didn't shake hands either, knowing that they were too weirdly soft to be male skateboarder hands. The group didn't seem to mind at all – in fact they seemed glad, not wanting to catch whatever it was that was making the Wong kid cough. They talked while Ming would occasionally nod.

Thirty minutes later a short overweight, balding man in shiny gray pants with a too tight purple golf shirt bearing a Sisu Soda logo strolled up to them. He was followed by a pretty woman who looked to be in her early twenties. She had short blond hair, was dressed extremely sharp and was lugging two briefcases and several small company gift bags.

"Hello kiddies! You must be the boarders. How can I tell? Well, don't ask, I'm Ira Golden your manager, chaperone and babysitter for this skateboarding boy-soda tour. This is my short term assistant *I hope* – Brie. I like to call her cheese. Feel free to do the same."

Brie nodded, smiled and gave a polite wave while quietly saying, "Brianna."

"Eh-hem!" Ira shot her a dirty look and continued as he paced in front of them, "There are two things that I expect from you, one – manners, and two – discipline! I am not supposed to be here, but unfortunately I got stuck on this happy little excursion. So, I will make this very short and sweet…I can make this tour extremely unpleasant for you. In fact, if you don't follow my rules I can, and I will, have you eliminated from the tour. Is that perfectly clear?"

The group slowly eyed each other, wondering if this guy was for real or joking.

"I said, is that clear?!"

They nodded in unison.

"Uh, I didn't hear you," Ira said snottily as he held his arms up.

"Yeah…Yes…Uh-huh…Sure dude…" the team replied.

"Good! Oh, and one last thing…Dude, Bro, Ira, Hey you," Ira said bobbing his head at them, "none of that will fly with me. You will refer to me as Mr. Golden," he turned and briskly snapped his fingers at Brie. She scrambled to hand out a gift bag to each one of them.

They were thrilled when they opened the bags to find they had each been given a quad phone.

"Far out!" said Harlo.

"This is totally cool!" agreed Donell.

But Ming just stared at Brie in shock.

"Yes, unlimited minutes and they work worldwide. But as cool as they may be, I expect to be able to reach each and every one of you at any time I please! And you are not to be out of my sight. Is that clear?" Ira insisted.

They nodded at him again, half excited about the phones, and half in shock at the meanness of their tour manager.

"Now then, let's have dinner shall we? We have a lot of rules to go over for the tour," Ira sneered. He began walking toward the hotel restaurant. Brie tottered behind him trying to keep up, while everyone hurried to follow.

"As I just said, I expect *all* of you to be with me at *all* times and you are not to be out of my sight," continued Ira.

"Are you saying we have to share a room with you?" Harlo joked, hoping to break the ice with the cold manager while clutching his laptop.

Ira stopped dead in his tracks and slowly turned around to face Harlo.

"No, laptop boy, and unless you plan on riding that, I suggest you ditch it!"

Harlo backed away grimacing, as Ira turned and continued walking. Donell then sarcastically made a face at Ira.

"And if you continue to make faces like children behind my back, I will treat you as such. Table for seven, and five childrens' menus please," Ira said to the Maitre'd, smirking.

When the waitress came to the table, Donell was the first to order.

"Uh, yeah, I'll have the Surf & Turf with a big sirloin and crab legs, a baked potato – everything on it, a salad with ranch and a bowl of clam chowder, with fresh baked bread, and a spinach cheese dip appetizer."

"What? I don't see any of that on the kid's menu," exclaimed Pal quickly scanning the menu for what Donell had just ordered.

"What exactly do you think you're doing?" asked Ira leaning in toward Donell.

"I'm sure you don't want your team weak, tired and hungry under your watch, man," Donell shot back sternly.

Ira glared at Donell and said nothing.

"Alrighty then!" said Pal as he happily ordered two full size meals. The rest of the table continued to do the same, ordering a ton of food, except for Ming.

"Ahhh, my kind of man!" Ira said to Ming as he finished ordering and closed the menu. But Ming glared at Ira, clearly showing her disgust with him.

The team laughed and talked about winning the competition, boarding, and the tour while Ira focused on his PDA.

When their food arrived, they ate like they had never eaten in their lives. A strong bond had begun to form between them, thanks to the nastiness of their manager.

Ira continued interjecting rude comments; like how completely sickened he was with their behavior. While he commanded Brie, "Cheese," as he'd rudely refer to her, to jot down any discrepancies.

It was clear that this tour was the last place Ira Golden wanted to be. He had been with the Sisu Soda company for five years and had been passed over for countless promotions and raises because of his superior, bossy attitude.

Ira had stolen his co-workers' ideas saying they were his. He criticized how things were done; always saying he could do better. When he blatantly insulted the female manager of his division with a chauvinistic remark, he had sealed his fate with the company.

Ira sat back, thinking how he wasn't supposed to be on this tour, he was supposed to have the corner office. He was extremely bitter, yet he didn't care. He enjoyed being rude and nasty, and was still determined to get promoted – no matter what it took.

The group continued enjoying themselves while ignoring him. By the end of the meal it was clear that Ira and Ming were the outsiders.

The next morning, everyone had to be in the lobby ready to catch the flight to London by 5:00 a.m. As tired as they were from staying up late, they were overwhelmed with excitement.

Ira had given them new shirts, bags, shoes, and boards with the Thrash Energy Drink logo on it. It was clear the gifts had come from the company; Ira would've kept them all to himself if he could have.

The best gifts of all were still the quad-band phones. Ira, again, made it clear to keep them turned on and charged at all times. He barked that if they weren't in their rooms, they better be with him or somewhere on the hotel premises in England.

Everyone pitched in to help load the enormous amount of luggage into the limo except Ira. Once it was loaded, the limo zoomed off to the airport.

80

They only things they had to worry about at the airport were their carry-on bags. Once seated on the plane, the flight attendant instructed Harlo that he had to put his laptop in the overhead compartment or under his seat. He defiantly said, "No."

"Sir, it is part of FAA regulations," the flight attendant insisted.

Harlo sat holding his laptop tightly while again shaking his head 'no.'

"Then I will have to ask you to de-board the plane, sir," the angry attendant snapped.

"Ohhh, is one of my little boys acting up again?" asked Ira as he walked up, "Put the darn computer under your seat for take-off now, King, or you are off this plane and tour!"

Reluctantly, Harlo obeyed. When they walked away, Pal, who was sitting next to Harlo asked, "What's so important about that laptop, dude?"

"It just makes me feel safe, being away from home and all. Plus, I can communicate with my friends," replied Harlo.

"Yeah, I get it, that's cool dude," nodded Pal.

"Besides, I recently got connected with this guy who is totally into the paranormal, just like I am. He knows everything about it," whispered Harlo.

"Oh, paranormal. You mean like Ira?" laughed Pal.

81

"Yeah, really dude. But it's actually ghosts and haunted places, spirits, the supernatural, stuff like that."

"Ooouuu! That stuff scares me, bro," said Pal seriously.

Just then, the pilot's voice came over the loudspeaker and Pal jumped.

"See what I mean! I'm hearing voices already."

"Ouuuuu…Ouuuuu….Ouuuuu!" teased Donell as he put his hands along the sides of Pal's seat from behind.

"Hey! I always thought ghosts were white!" joked Pal.

"Not where I'm from!" laughed Donell.

"Listen to the pilot, kiddies!" snapped Ira from across the aisle.

As the plane took off, they began to read and listen to music. Once the plane had reached its altitude, Harlo pulled out his computer and turned it on. He was excited he was able to connect with GT. GT had already told him about some of the haunted castles in England to check out. There was one he was especially adamant about. He insisted that Harlo go see Castle Cloon de Sade.

When Harlo wrote back saying he would if he had time, or if he could manage to get away from Ira…GT seemed irritated. He stated that it was something Harlo *must do*! A little surprised by his insistence, Harlo wrote that he would try and signed off.

82

A few hours later, after lunch, Ira informed everyone he did not want to be bothered. Not to wake him up unless it was an emergency, and by emergency he meant something wrong with the plane, not them.

"Until we land, you are to stay in your assigned seats and be good boys!" said Ira putting his head on a pillow.

Everyone ignored him, including Ming who had now moved to the seat next to Brie.

"Don't I know you?" Ming quietly questioned Brie.

"I don't think so," said Brie, scrunching her face while she continued to read her magazine.

"Okay, don't freak out or anything, but do you remember the agent, Sam Handler?" asked Ming with her hat pulled down.

Brie stopped reading and stared suspiciously at Ming.

"He always called you for the exact same audition as an Asian girl…The two of you became friends. You always thought it was so weird because you looked like total opposites and laughed about being called for the exact same auditions and parts…The other girl had long black hair…" Ming continued.

"Don't tell me you're her brother?!" Brie asked excitedly, "We lost contact when I dropped that bum of an agent and got out of acting."

"No…shhhhh," said Ming, "Now, don't freak out. But...I'm her."

Brie contorted her face as if she was completely grossed out. Ming was afraid that one of the other guys in front of them was going to hear them…but just then…

"Hey, guys! Look what I got in the bag of snacks my mom packed for me!" said Harlo kneeling in his seat as he held up a tattoo of a pink kitten.

"Oh, how sweet!" said Terrence.

"Can I have one, too?" smirked Donell.

"No! Shhhhh…I've got an idea!" He said, pointing to Ira, who was now sound asleep.

They all laughed while silently giving Harlo a thumb's up.

Pal handed Harlo his water to soak the tattoo in. Once it was ready, Harlo blotted it dry and they silently moved over to sleeping Ira. Harlo quickly put the tattoo on Ira's forehead. Since Ira was folded over in his seat, Donell gently placed Ira's arm over his head to hold it in place.

Ming and Brie could see they were doing something to sleeping Ira, but knew he deserved it. He reminded Ming of her agent, 'or former agent,' she thought to herself. An overbearing rude phony!

Ming continued to explain the entire story to Brie. Brie couldn't believe her ears and began laughing out loud, causing the rest of the team to turn and stare at them. It was clear by the looks on their faces they couldn't believe that Ming was actually talking! Let alone to a hot girl like Brie, and making her laugh!

Brie and Ming tried to stop laughing when they saw them staring. When everyone went back to what they were doing, Ming finished the story. Brie agreed to keep Ming's secret, happy that they were back in touch and that she now had a friend on the tour.

The others were trying to suppress their laughter when the flight attendant moved the beverage cart past Ira.

After a nine-hour flight, the plane landed safely at Heathrow Airport in England. The group gathered their gear to deplane. But every time they looked at Ira, it was impossible to contain themselves!

They followed him off the plane and through the airport completely amused. Every time Ira barked out orders the little pink kitty on his forehead would move! It began causing mass hysteria with the team. People walking past Ira would just stare at him.

When they arrived at the baggage claim, Ira told them to wait together while he went to the men's room.

A few minutes later he stormed out of the men's room toward them, furious!

"Very, very funny, whose clever little idea was this?" he barked angrily.

They tried suppressing their laughter, which only made them laugh harder.

"That's enough!" he screamed.

They froze.

"If you don't tell me who did this, you will all pay."

"I did," said Harlo as he moved forward.

"You won't skate at the showing tomorrow!" snapped Ira.

"You can't do that!" said Harlo.

"I can and I will! I am not here to play games with immature idiots!" hollered Ira.

"If you aren't into boarding and the tour then why are you here period?" asked Pal stepping forward.

Ira began yelling at Pal, when Terrence stepped forward. He interrupted Ira's yelling saying that if Harlo doesn't ride, then he wouldn't either. One by one, they all stood up to Ira saying the same thing, except for Ming.

As Ira turned to Ming smiling, she kept her head down and shook it 'no.'

"Not you either, huh? Alright, alright, if this is how you want to play, we'll see who wins this game!" barked Ira.

Ira was outnumbered and he knew it.

Twenty-two
The Murder

"NOOOOOOOOO!!!" The maid's scream could be heard for miles.

The servants ran to the ballroom where the terrifying scream had come from. There, in the middle of the ballroom, was a bloody pile of bodies! The Duchess and the twins were dead!

"Get to town and find the sheriff!" yelled the butler, "and you! Try to find the Duke!"

The horrified servants scurried about in complete shock!

Red blood poured out of the slumped over bodies, covering a huge area of the black and white checked tile floor. It was a grisly, tragic site!

The servants couldn't imagine who could commit such a dreadful murder. When they had left that day for their trip to town, all was normal and quiet within the massive castle. There hadn't even been bickering among the twins. The Duchess was happily doing her needlework, while, as always, the Duke was counting his money -- even though he hadn't paid them in weeks.

As they anxiously searched the castle, they could find no sign of intruders, but the Duke's vault was open and empty. So, whoever committed such an evil crime, had also robbed the family!

When the coroner and the law arrived, they spent the entire day searching the castle for clues. The servants and villagers hunted in desperation for the Duke, but he was nowhere to be found. Even his horse was missing. They were afraid he was so angered and distressed at the site of the murder that he might have gone after the villain.

As the day wore on, things grew more and more disturbing as the villagers grew terrified. Never had anything so gruesome happened in the town of Twickenshire. The town was aghast that such a crime could have taken place in their fair village, yet nobody pined for the loss of the Cloon de Sade family. More so, they wondered what had happened to the cruel Duke. They speculated whether he had run away, or been kidnapped and held ransom for his riches.

Even more horrifying was when the haunting began at the castle that very same night! Shocking screams and groans seemed to come from the walls! It was so frightening that the servants fled immediately!

From that day on, nobody could stay in the castle, and many times people tried. The vicious event had left restless spirits to roam and terrorize what was once one of the most magnificent castles in the country.

The murder of the Duchess, Addison and Alistair, along with the disappearance of the Duke, left so many unanswered questions for the once peaceful village that the town of Twickenshire would never be the same again.

Twenty-three
The London Hotel

The limousine pulled up to the stately brick hotel. It was just blocks away from bustling Piccadilly Circus and, since it was night time, the glowing neon added to the excitement of being in London. But it quickly wore off, thanks to nasty Ira.

They got their bags and checked in to their rooms. Ira informed them they were free to order room service; it was too late for dinner.

They secretly decided to meet in Harlo and Pal's room in fifteen minutes, but they weren't going to invite Ming. For some reason, he just didn't fit in with the group.

Terrence felt bad, since he had to share a room with Ming. He would have to find a way to sneak out.

"Uhhh…feel free to order dinner or whatever, I'm gonna go, uh… look around," Terrence said, feeling bad the minute the words came out of his mouth. All he could think of was what kind of bad Karma was going to happen to him for lying so much lately! He despised lying.

"You're not supposed to leave the room," said Mingmei in her fake voice, although inside she was relieved.

With Terrence gone she could take her hat off and relax, without having to sit around in disguise.

"Yeah, I know. Hey, you spoke!" said Terrence.

"Yeah, so what? I'm just quiet," said Ming smugly.

"Cool, that's like totally cool. So look, you don't mind, do ya?" asked Terrence.

Ming shook her head 'no.' She figured they were all getting together and didn't care. The more she was an outcast from the team, the easier it would be for her.

Terrence left the room, quietly pulling the heavily carved door shut. He carefully moved down the ornate hallway. The entire hotel was done in the Victorian era. It featured high tin covered ceilings and the walls were papered in a busy floral pattern. Every piece of furniture was covered in rich velvet or brocade fabric and the colors were deep reds, purples, and blues. It was totally different from the hotel in California, but just as impressive in its own way.

It reminded him of some kind of old English castle, the kind he had seen in pictures. What Terrence didn't know was just how soon he would actually be in one!

Terrence quietly tapped on Pal's door.

"What's the password?" asked Pal from the other side of the door.

"What? I don't know," said Terrence, suddenly startled by a tall figure that loomed up next to him.

"Did you knock?" asked Donell unexpectedly.

91

"Hey, don't sneak up on me like that!" said Terrence shuddering.

"Oh, sorry man," said Donell.

"They won't let me in without a password!" said Terrence.

Just as Donell was about to knock, they heard a door opening two rooms down. Ira was coming out of his hotel room!

"Duck!" said Donell as they quickly crouched behind a wooden desk that was next to them.

"Open up! Ira in the hall! IRA IN THE HALL!" Terrence whispered fiercely under his breath.

"That's it! How did you know?" laughed Pal as he opened up the door and looked out. Upon seeing Ira, Pal quickly leaned back into the room and began to close the door, until he felt someone pushing on it! Terrence and Donell began to crawl past Pal's feet, as he moved to let them in. He then carefully peeked out again to see Ira standing at the elevator. Pal slowly and quietly closed the door.

"That jerk is going out to dinner!" said Pal angrily.

"That's not fair," mumbled Harlo from his computer.

"Password? Like, what the heck?" asked Terrence.

"I was just joking," shrugged Pal.

They talked about how to get around Ira as they

92

ordered room service.

"Harlo, get off your computer and help us figure this out!" said Donell.

"Yeah, why are you always on that thing?" asked Terrence.

"I'm reading about haunted places in England," replied Harlo. He began to tell them how, in one castle, a maid roams the halls with blood-stained towels in her hands. In another haunted place, a gray ghost of a man with maggots coming out of his head wanders around knocking on doors while turning on and off lights. Harlo continued telling them gory, violent ghost stories until…

KNOCK, KNOCK, KNOCK!! They all jumped!

Luckily it was room service and it took their minds off the scary tales. The attendant's rolled in five tables of food.

"That's not all," continued Harlo as they began uncovering the plates of food.

"But sir, this is everything you ordered!" said one of the room service attendants.

"No, I mean about the ghosts…" laughed Harlo as the man's face grew pale with fear. He shoved the bill at them, Pal signed it and they quickly left the room.

Donell insisted that was enough scary storytelling for him, but Harlo persisted. Finally they heard him out. He told them GT had told him there was a castle not too far from where they were staying, just about 40 minutes outside the city. It was abandoned and haunted and if they wanted, they could sneak in.

By now, everyone was too busy eating to pay attention. The conversation shifted to deciding what kind of plan they could come up with to torment evil Ira.

Twenty-four
Short Sheet

"I've got it!" yelled Pal.

"What?" they asked in unison.

"Short sheet!" he yelled, as he began to explain, "You take the top sheet off the bed, fold the sheet in half and tuck it back in tightly toward the top of the bed. Then you fold it back over the blanket, so it looks like the bed is made up normally. When someone tries to get in to the bed, they can't get their feet in!"

They decided it was the perfect, harmless joke. After eating, they called and asked for turndown service for Ira's room from a quad phone. That way the front desk couldn't see the room number they were calling from. Peering out the door, Donell watched for the evening maid.

He gave a thumbs-up and quickly tiptoed out to put a piece of skateboard grip tape across the lock of Ira's room door, so that it wouldn't lock when the maid left. He rushed back before the maid came out.

They watched silently from Pal's door. Finally, the maid left Ira's room! They crept down the hall. Donell gave Ira's door a shove – it creaked open!

Terrence and Harlo quickly short sheeted the bed, while Pal called out instructions. Donell kept watch at the door. It was done! While leaving Ira's room, Donell added a little something more to the joke; he turned the thermostat to heat - high!

"That is just awesome!" Harlo went to high-five Donell.

"They don't do that high five crap where I come from!" snapped Donell angrily as they all froze looking at Donell.

"Ha ha! Gotcha! Just kiddin'!" said Donell as he high-five'd back. They laughed and knew they would be great friends for a long, long time.

"Well, I don't know about you, but I'm tired," Terrence sighed.

"Hey, by the way, what's up with your roomie, Ming?" questioned Pal.

"Kinda weird – huh?" asked Harlo.

"I don't know, just quiet I guess," responded Terrence, "See you guys tomorrow."

By the time Terrence got back to the room, Ming was fast asleep – with his hat on. Terrence decided that the guys were right. Ming was weird. He began to wonder how his mother was as he drifted off to sleep.

Donell was lucky enough to have his own room. He wanted to call his family again, but he had already spoken to them four times since the trip began. He felt like he was a million miles away and decided to write a letter, but fell asleep at Dear…

Pal finished eating everyone's leftover food, while Harlo wrapped up the night with another instant message.

"I can't believe you're still hungry," stated Harlo.

"Yeah, I have room for it," said Pal as he belched loudly and smiled rubbing his belly. "I can't believe you have so much to say to this guy…and that he never sleeps. Where is he anyway?"

"I dunno," answered Harlo, "but he insists that we visit this one castle…" The two continued talking about ghosts until Pal started to get afraid. He insisted they go to sleep, with the light on and Harlo agreed.

"AGGGGGHHHHHH!" Pal and Harlo sat upright from their sound sleep.

It was one o'clock in the morning and the horrible screams startled them awake!

The yelling reverberated through the entire floor of the hotel.

"Ohhhh…It's Ira! Listen!" whispered Pal yawning.

"You're right! Great idea on the short-sheeting," snickered Harlo.

"Just a little teamwork…night, bro," replied Pal as he covered his head with his pillow and went back to sleep.

Twenty-five
Madman Ira

The next morning at breakfast, they discussed the upcoming day. It was calm and peaceful until Ira angrily stormed into the dining room. He was a mess. His hair was tousled and he was unshaven, his shirt was half tucked in and his collar stood up on one side. He yanked out a chair and plopped himself down at the table.

They were silent as they watched his hands shake while he wiped them across his face. He took a deep breath and spoke as sternly and angrily as he possibly could.

"How did you, you jerks get in my room last night?" he insisted.

"Whaz up, Ira, my man?" asked Pal.

"Good morning to you, too! Sleep well?" asked Donell chewing on a pastry.

Ira slammed his fist down and they jumped. The other diners turned and stared at the disturbance.

"I will have you off this tour just like that!" Ira said snapping his fingers.

"No. Don't think so. Uh-uh," the group replied while they continued to eat.

"You see, Ira, it goes like this; you don't really want to be here. Right? Am I right or am I right? So, that tells us if anyone would be leavin' our fun little tour then it would be you!" stated Pal calmly.

"My man, Pal, here is right," insisted Donell.

"Yeah, it's true, we know your story, man," Terrence joined in.

The arguing began to escalate until Ming stood up and threw her napkin onto her plate. Again she was wearing her hat and a Sisu Soda shirt that was at least five sizes to big for her and bulky looking.

"I think this is about enough!" she said in her weird voice, "We are here representing the United States and this beverage company! And whether we see eye-to-eye or not, if we don't start getting along, it will affect the entire tour and we will all lose!"

Everyone was silent as Ming stared at Ira's face.

They nodded in agreement except for Ira. Instead he picked up his juice, drank it down, got up and stormed out of the restaurant to the lobby. Brie shook her head and rolled her eyes at Ira, as she quickly followed him out.

"Why's he gotta be like that? Last night was just a little joke," said Harlo.

"Nobody has a sense of humor anymore," insisted Pal grabbing a pancake off Terrence's plate when he wasn't looking.

"Well, at least you guys have a sense of humor," said Ming.

They were again shocked that she was talking as they became silent, until a piece of toast tumbled out of Harlo's open mouth. Then they all started laughing hysterically.

It was clear that Ira was still aggravated with everyone as he angrily motioned for them to join him in the lobby. He instructed them to get their gear and boards and to be in the limousine in ten minutes.

Twenty-six
A Photo Session

The limo left the hotel, twisting and turning through the winding streets of London as their driver pointed out landmarks. When they arrived at London's West End, the team was in awe of the magnificent city and some of the monuments they had just seen.

They were dropped off on a skinny side street lined with brightly colored studios, shops, galleries and cafés. They followed Ira through purple painted doors into a three-story red brick building. Once inside, they were amazed at the totally cool photo studio.

It was a wide open space all the way up to the top story on the inside. A metal circular stairway curved upstairs, with a thick wood railing that wrapped all the way around leading to the second and third levels.

They were quickly introduced to three impeccably dressed and very proper men and a woman from the English division of Sisu Soda. They shook hands and welcomed them to London, while offering any assistance they might need while there.

Terrence noticed a strange moment when the woman shook Ming's hand. The woman stared at him oddly for a second then continued greeting everyone else.

The team was given a tour of the trendy studio. The walls were white, with super modern furniture. Even though they had just eaten, there was an enormous cart filled with soda, fruit, candy, cakes, cookies, and other delicious items for snacking. It didn't take Pal long to find his way to the cart, as he called his friends to join him.

It seemed like every major celebrity on the planet had visited the studio. There was a massive wall where there were pictures of celebrities, musicians, models, dignitaries, and even politicians, and they had all autographed it.

While eating cookies and drinking Thrash Energy Drinks, five personal assistants came over to them with a marker to have them sign the wall.

"No kidding? Yeah, I'll stop eating cookies for that!" exclaimed Pal.

"Yeah, mates, you are now celebrities yourselves!" said one of the executives.

"That sounds cool to me 'eh mates…" Harlo said, trying out his best English accent imitation.

After signing the wall, they were escorted by their assistants to the private dressing rooms to change into designer outfits for the photo session.

Their hair was styled and makeup was put on them. When they came out of the dressing rooms, they were shocked. They couldn't believe how great they were made to look! Especially Terrence, he was definitely the model of the group.

They joked and laughed as they posed on the cool Thrash Energy Drink set. There were tons of props; gigantic skateboards, snowboards, surfboards, mountain boards and huge soda cans. There was even an enormous screen that the photographer called the green screen. Depending on what they were shooting at the time, they could project anything from ocean waves, to a stadium with millions of people on the screen. The entire photo session was a blast!

Terrence began to notice that every time they had to change into a new outfit, Ming would grab the clothes and bolt away from his assistant. Ming argued that he could not be photographed without his trademark hat on. After a heavy discussion with the executives, they gave in. The only exception was that in the final photos they would have to superimpose a Thrash Energy Drink logo on the hat. Ming happily agreed.

Terrence didn't say anything to the other guys, since they didn't like Ming as it was, but he couldn't help but wonder what Ming's problem was.

Twenty-seven
The First Demo

Once finished, a quick demo with an autograph session was planned at the Wembley Arena. It was just a pre-show appearance where the world tour kickoff would launch.

When they arrived at the arena they couldn't believe the masses of people in line, and they were mostly girls! There were news cameras and paparazzi buzzing about. Vendors were selling photos and t-shirts of them! Pictures that had been taken in the United States on the day they won the competition!

"This must be how rock stars feel and I'm diggin' it!" said Donell excitedly.

"Yeah, well don't *dig* it too long! In this business you're already toast," barked Ira as he opened the limo door and began to walk down the red carpet ahead of them. He waved for them to follow him. The area was roped off so that they could walk through as fans yelled and screamed for their attention!

"Yeah, well, don't dig it too long…in this business you're already toast, no wait, maybe you're a muffin, no, better yet – a waffle…" joked Donell mimicking Ira's voice and actions as they followed behind him laughing and waving at the enormous crowd.

Ming waved slowly as she followed the group. It felt odd to her pretending to be a boy like this. She couldn't believe she had pulled it off this long. She had to make it through the first show and then she would be in for the long haul. After that it would be nearly impossible for them to replace her without a scandal. No beverage company wanted that in the newspapers. This was the role of a lifetime for her, a really tough role.

Ming moved down the red carpet while copying how the guys acted and walked.

'C'mon, Ming, you're a better actress than this! You have to really play it up! Walk like them, pose like them, you can do it...' she thought to herself. Out of the corner of her eye she caught Brie turn and shoot her a look that said *get with the program and act!*

Ming quickly snapped out of it, but she couldn't help notice Terrence shaking girl's hands. There was one girl who wouldn't let go of him until the bodyguards came to his rescue and forced her apart. Terrence was graceful about it; but, for some reason, it irritated Ming. There was something about Terrence. Maybe it was because he was kinder to her than the rest of the team. Either way, she knew she'd better focus on her acting.

They entered the arena and were escorted to the platform. The place was amazing. The set-up was as cool as the X-Games, but more compact with the vert ramp right next to the street course. A popular local band was jamming as they warmed up and readied themselves for their first skating demo.

Once the crowd was seated and the MC began, they took their place at the top of the giant vert ramp.

"Man, if this is what it's like when we're unknown, just imagine how Tony feels!" said Pal excitedly.

"No kidding!" agreed Donell.

"Yeah, I think it's just the beginning!" said Harlo.

"Welcome to Wembley Arena! This is just a little demo session to get you jazzed for the real stuff – Sisu Soda's Thrash Energy Drink, Challenge Yourself Because You'll be Challenged World Tour kickoff! Welcome our skaters from America…"

The audience roared as each of them waved when their names were announced and then began to ride. They had a blast on the super high vert! At one point, three of them were riding at once! The crowd went wild! The team loved being in the limelight, and agreed that -- even though it was a short ride -- it felt good to be back boarding again!

"Man, that was just gnarly!" shouted Harlo as they bowed and took off their helmets.

"Fashizzle!!!" shouted Donell cracking up.

106

"Sick, I tell ya! Sick!" said Terrence.

"Yeah man, it was off the hook!" Ming agreed.

"My bros, we rock!" said Pal as they shook hands, bowed again, and patted each other on the back.

The team picked up their gear together and were escorted to the entrance area to sign autographs. There were tables set up and bodyguards. Sisu Soda employees were getting people in line. Paparazzi were flashing pictures every chance they could, while reporters tried to interview them.

It seemed like the lines were endless; everyone from boys wanting their boards signed to flirting girls. People asked them all kinds of questions, "When did they start skateboarding? Did they like London? Where were there families?" Strangers even asked them what their favorite colors were.

Numerous times the bodyguards and Sisu Soda employees had to step in and move the girls away from the table to keep the crowd moving. Especially from Pal, he kept trying to get the phone number of every girl that went by. Three hours later, they were finally finished.

Twenty-eight
Touring the Bottling Plant

"Man, that was wild!" said Pal still full of energy.

"Yeah, do you think those people were there for the free stuff Sisu was handing out?" Harlo questioned.

"Maybe, but who cares? I am tiiiiired," answered Donell.

"Tired? Are ya? Huh, Dread Head?" prodded Ira, "ya tired?"

"Dread head, I like that!" laughed Pal while Donell nodded and winked at Ira.

"Think your funny, huh?" continued Ira, "all my little joke playing boys tired?"

They looked at him suspiciously, wondering what he was up to.

"Well, that's just too bad! Because I planned a three-hour tour of the local Sisu Soda plant just for you! Ha! We'll see who short sheets who tonight!" Ira laughed evilly.

"Aw, c'mon, Ira, take a joke, man!" said Harlo.

"Yeah, at least let us go for a little rest and recuperation. You know, to be ready for the party," pleaded Terrence.

"Not a chance, my little lovelies," grinned Ira.

As they began to head toward the limo, Pal said under his breath, "Man, he's trippy!"

"You can say that again," said Donell.

"Man, he's trippy," said Pal.

They were whisked away to the Sisu Company bottling plant just outside London. Once there, they were given a tour of the entire plant. They actually enjoyed seeing their new favorite drink being made and bottled. And they filled themselves with free samples, determined not to let Ira think for a second that they weren't enjoying themselves. It was apparent that Ira was far more bored than they were, so his little devious plan had backfired.

When the tour was over, they were led to an enormous board room. In the center of the room was a huge, oval cherry table with high back leather chairs around it. One side of the room was floor to ceiling windows with a magnificent view overlooking miles of England.

They were asked to take a seat as the executives briefed them on how to promote the Sisu Soda Company when they were interviewed by the press. They had noticed that some of them had put their faces right up to the cameras on the live news feed at the arena. They had said things like, "Sisu is gnarly!" and "Thrash Energy Drink is sick!"

They understood that the word 'sick' meant cool to them, but it just didn't quite work for the company image. They wanted them to try being a bit more diplomatic.

The team nodded as they looked at each other, trying to keep from bursting out laughing.

"I've been trying to work with them on that, but they are showing their age," chirped Ira.

"It's understandable," said the woman, "It's their first tour. I always tell headquarters that this should be done prior to their meeting with the public. They'll get the hang of it."

"They must've forgotten that we're sitting right here," Donell whispered to Terrence sarcastically.

The executives met with each of them individually, explaining the upcoming boarding workshops. They talked about what they expected for the 'Challenge Yourself Because You'll be Challenged!' segment of the tour. And about their individual boarding experience and what they felt their strongest tricks were.

When they were ready to go, the executives explained that the next stop on the tour would be unveiled at the kickoff. Everyone tried to get it out of them, but they said it was top secret.

"Where would you like to go, Ming?" asked the woman executive abruptly. Shocked by the question being directed right at her, Ming started her fake cough while saying, "Cough…I, cough, cough, don't cough really know."

The room grew quiet at the strangeness of the moment.

"I say somewhere sunny, it's a little gray here!" said Terrence, and everyone joined in and agreed as a discussion started on the bleak skies and how much rain they get in London.

Terrence did it on purpose, and was glad he did when he saw Ming look at him gratefully. It was almost as if he was starting to look out for the strange fellow.

"Harlo, tell me you aren't going to steal any of our company's secrets," said one of the executives as he motioned to Harlo's laptop, which Harlo was holding onto tightly.

"No, not soda. Ghosts maybe, but not soda," Harlo laughed.

"We do have one last surprise for you," said another executive as he pushed a button on the side of the table.

Almost immediately an elderly woman in a gray suit appeared. She was carrying a silver tray lined with five small black leather boxes. She stopped at each one of them and let them take the box with their name on it.

"We were going to give you these at the kickoff, but since you were gracious enough to visit us, we wanted you to have them now. Just a little good luck present for beginning your tour with us!" said the other executive.

As they opened their boxes they yelled with delight! Each one had been given a beautiful platinum ring. The ring featured a small design of four different engraved boards; a skateboard, a surfboard, a snowboard and a mountainboard centered around an S for Sisu with a small diamond in the middle. The rings fit each of them perfectly!

"So, this is why they measured our dang fingers at the contest!" said Donell.

"Far out!" said Terrence.

"Uh, yeah, thanks!" Ming joined in.

After shaking hands and thanking them, the team was escorted back to the limo. It was clear that Ira was totally agitated, since he didn't get a ring. He sat silently stewing the entire ride back to the hotel.

Twenty-nine
Wrong Room

The site of the hotel made them happy to be back. It had been a long day and they were exhausted.

Ira instructed them to get cleaned up for the 'Meet and Greet' in the Sedworth Ballroom promptly at 7:00 p.m. There would be a few celebrities, local politicians and more Sisu Soda execs. He tensely instructed them to wear the new Sisu apparel that had been sent up to their rooms.

"That's cool, dude!" said Pal.

"Hey! What did I tell you about calling me dude? And don't be late! This is an important event for you children! Uh-uh, Cheese, you come with me, we have some things to take care of," barked Ira as Brie climbed back into the limo.

"Poor thing," said Ming. It seemed like Ming had formed a unique friendship with Brie.

"I think Ming has a thing for Brie…" whispered Harlo to Terrence as they walked ahead of Ming through the lobby.

"Nahhh…no way," replied Terrence, even though he had began to wonder the same thing himself.

Ming had overheard their whispering and thought to herself what idiots they were not to realize that she could hear them. But she knew she better watch how chummy she was with Brie. She didn't want them to become too inquisitive or suspicious. Besides Brie was a good ally to have.

When they got to their rooms, their doors wouldn't open! Not one of their keys worked! Abruptly, Terrence and Ming's door flew open. A gruff older man with gray hair and a large handlebar moustache stood there irritated.

"May I help you?" He bellowed.

Terrence and Ming looked at him shocked. The grumpy old man was standing there in red and white striped boxers with a white tank t-shirt and ridiculous looking knee garters holding up his short black socks with shiny black dress shoes on!

"Like, ummm, sorry to bother you, sir," Terrence said averting his eyes, "but I believe this is our room."

"Ehhh-hem…Your room? Well, I believe you are quite wrong, bloke!" The man replied rudely. "Now, if you would be so kind as to not disturb me, in *my* room, again!" He slammed the door in their faces.

A second later a woman peeked out of the room that Harlo and Pal had been in! She screamed, "Strange men are at the door, Irving!"

114

A man nudged the woman out of the way and asked what was going on.

Harlo excused himself by saying that they must have the wrong room.

"Dude, what is going on?" Pal whispered to Harlo as they walked toward Terrence and Ming.

Donell immediately stopped trying to get into his room after the turmoil.

"I don't know, but we only have twenty minutes to get cleaned up and get back downstairs," said Harlo.

They went back downstairs to the front desk where the manager in charge insisted that their stay at the hotel was over. He said his records indicated that they checked out early that morning. Time was running out; even Ming argued with the man, but it was no use.

"Ha, ha, ha! Ha, ha, ha, ha, ha, ha!" They looked at each other when they heard the irritating laugh come from behind them.

"Ira!" said Terrence angrily.

They turned around to see Ira sitting smugly across from them on a sofa. He sat with his legs crossed and his arms folded, laughing hysterically; their luggage surrounding him.

"That'll teach you to mess with Ira Golden! Now, won't it?" He laughed as he stood up and walked to the front desk. He then whipped a fifty dollar bill out of his wallet, and slyly handed it to the man they had just argued with!

"Thank you, Nigel!" Ira said looking at his watch. He handed them each new room keys then barked, "Don't ever mess with me again, boys! You've got fifteen minutes till the Meet and Greet. I strongly suggest that you be in the Sedworth Ballroom on time!"

They scurried to pick up their luggage as Ira handed them their evening attire.

"He's a jackass!" said Terrence as he angrily pounded the elevator button.

"Yeah, game's on, Ira! You dork!" said Pal. This was the first time they'd seen Pal angry.

"Yeah, well he doesn't know who he's messin' with. That trick he just pulled was evil compared to our little pranks!" said Donell.

They nodded in agreement. Ming was the only one who was quiet, but silently fuming at the ridiculousness of their manager.

Thirty
Meet & Greet

They raced to their new rooms and got ready as fast as possible. They decided the best thing would be for them to show up as a team, better late together.

"C'mon! Let's go! What are you guys doing?!" Pal, Donell and Harlo yelled as they pounded on Terrence and Ming's door.

"Sorry," said Terrence opening up the door while buttoning his shirt. "Ming hogs the bathroom all the time."

Ming hurried out of the bathroom with her hat on, completely dressed. The team ran down five flights of stairs to the event. Completely out of breath, they entered the ballroom – ten minutes late.

They walked toward Ira, who was standing with a powerful looking man. Ira apologized for their tardiness, and declared that he was having trouble keeping them in line. He then introduced them one by one to the president of the English division of Sisu Soda.

"Well, mates, it's a pleasure to meet you. Let's just hope you respect your manager and you aren't late for the really big event. Constant tardiness shows lack of respect for the tour, and it could get you kicked off," said the president.

They nodded and politely apologized for being late. They hated Ira now more than ever. They moved around the room following Ira through introductions. They gasped when Ira approached another man.

Ira introduced him as Lord Montague, "I do believe as Americans, it is important that you display utmost respect at all times!" said the gray haired man. It was the same man who answered the door in his boxer shorts and t-shirt!

There was nothing they could do but look down or away, embarrassed, they were seething as they watched Ira smirking at them.

The party wore on into the night and they forgot about the entire mess. They mingled with a few American celebrities who were in England for filming; as well as famous English actors. They got autographs, ate from a sumptuous buffet and posed for pictures. It was the official send off party for the head honchos and the tour.

Pal fell in love numerous times throughout the evening; and it was nearly impossible to get Donell away from a beautiful English girl.

When the fun party ended, the team made sure they said a polite thank you and goodnight to everyone, except Ira.

It was the middle of the night when they were again startled awake up by someone yelling in the hallway! Pal and Harlo opened their door to peek out. So did Donell, Terrence and numerous other people from their rooms.

There was Ira, drunk, screaming, cursing and kicking his door.

"You did this! You did this!" he said screaming and turning to look around the hallway. Just then a massive man opened Ira's hotel door and grabbed him by the throat. He pushed Ira against the wall!

"Help me, you idiots!" choked Ira, but nobody moved.

"I believe you are at the wrong suite, little man! Now, get lost!" the massive Englishman said as he dropped Ira to the ground and went back to his room. People quickly shut their doors. The team was laughing hysterically; even Brie.

Ira scrambled to his feet and ran to Brie's door just as she slammed it in his face.

"I need help! Open up, Brie! That's an order!" Ira pounded.

Once again, the massive man opened his door and yelled, "Get out of here you little pest, before I tear you apart!" at which point Ira went screaming down the stairs!

The next day everyone was at breakfast except Ira. Brie explained that when he had pulled the 'switching the room trick,' the front desk had mistakenly changed his room, too!

Harlo laughed so hard that milk came out his nose! This made everyone at the table laugh even harder, until Ira showed up. The rest of the breakfast they ate in silence, trying hard to fight back the laughter.

Thirty-one
Sightseeing

The entire day they had to go on sightseeing tours of England. Ira was relentless. He made sure they saw every garden, right down to the last English rose. They went from St. Paul's Cathedral and the Museum of London, to the Tower of London and Madame Tussaud's Wax Museum. Ira insisted it would help his career as they built better English and American relations.

When they were halfway through Buckingham Palace, Ira had enough. He instructed Brie to stay with them and he would pick them up at the exit.

Ming continued walking ahead with Brie. When the coast was clear, Harlo and Pal quickly grabbed Donell and Terrence by their shirts pulling them against a wall.

They decided that if they ever wanted to see England on their own, or do any boarding, this would be their only chance to escape. They quickly ditched out a side exit, pulled their boards out of their backpacks and began to ride toward the closest bridge. The streets were crowded, providing more of a challenge as they grinded down rails, ollied up curbs and sped through the crowds.

They crossed a bridge over the River Thames and were in awe of the London Eye. It was a gigantic Ferris wheel, the biggest they'd ever seen! It was so huge that it had little pods on it that would hold entire groups of people.

Heading back, they crossed another bridge, and continued moving toward Piccadilly Circus. They zoomed past Big Ben and other beautiful monuments, while carefully dodging pedestrians.

At Piccadilly Circus they rode around the Eros Fountain and stopped. There were huge electric signs thrown against a backdrop of stunning old English buildings. Five streets filled with traffic intersected into the busy area. It was one of the coolest places they had ever seen!

"What are we waiting for?" asked Terrence, "let's go!"

They took off their helmets and picked up their boards and walked through the diverse group of people. It was a crazy scene with every nationality and all types of people; from punkers to models, business people to tourists.

Thirsty from boarding, they stopped at an outdoor café and ordered a Thrash Energy drink.

"I kinda feel bad about ditching Ming, ya know, leavin' him with Brie," said Terrence.

"Ahh, Ming's tore up," said Donell.

"Yeah, he doesn't even try to fit in. Besides I'm sure he doesn't mind being with Brie," exclaimed Pal.

"What'd ya mean by that?" asked Harlo.

"Why do you care? You got a thing for that little Blondie Brie, don't cha? I knew it! I saw the way you looked at her!" pried Donell.

"No way!" blushed Harlo, "She's too old for me, so forgettaboutit! I got a thing for ghosts…c'mon you really want to have some fun?"

Harlo started to talk about seeing the old haunted castle that his friend GT had told him about. Tired, they knew they should get back to the hotel. But Harlo's story was too tempting. It would be their only chance to escape from Ira, and it sounded like fun. The more Harlo told them about the mysterious castle, the more interested they became. Finally, he talked them into going!

Thirty-two
The Cab Ride

They hailed a cab and jumped in. Harlo popped open his laptop while giving the cabbie directions.

"You mean we're goin' where your instant message buddy from the States keeps tellin' you to go?" asked Donell inquisitively, as the cab winded down the roads leading out of the city.

Harlo nodded excitedly.

"Well, that's just crazy, man!" laughed Donell, "almost as crazy as me bein' in London, England, skateboardin' and rich!"

"Talk about rich, wait 'til I tell you this story…" Harlo began to tell them how the haunted castle had been built in the 1700s… "By one of the wealthiest men in England, Duke Cloon De Sade. It was one of the grandest castles in all of Europe. The finest cherry and walnut woods were imported and carved to perfection to line the walls. Marble was imported from Italy, and the most exquisite fabrics from around the world were hand woven for curtains and draping. The best of everything was used, the finest crystal chandeliers, pewter and gold fittings. Even diamond shaped glass window panes were installed, at an enormous expense."

"Okay, get to the scary part already," insisted Pal.

"I am, dude…Okay, who farted?" asked Harlo.

They all looked at Pal as he grinned.

"Oh, dude, that's vile!" said Terrence rolling down the window.

"So, anyway this guy is super wealthy and really ruthless in business," continued Harlo as he waved the smell away. "He had some enemies, so to protect his family from intruders, there were six enormous towers, plus a wall and gatehouse built around this gigantic castle. They even say he had a torture chamber in the dungeon, just in case anybody did break in or if someone really made him mad.

This guy wanted his family, his wife and twin sons, Addison and Alistair to have an idyllic place to live. When his sons were young, they always had huge parties at the castle, and they attended every important event in England, especially sporting and hunting events, which he made sure his sons were a part of.

But the sons were like bad seeds, always arguing. As they grew older, they grew competitive with each other. The Duke and Duchess gave them everything, but no matter what, these evil twins became more and more jealous of each other.

At parties they would break out in fist fights. Every public event they would quarrel. The fighting got so bad that the Duke and Duchess were totally humiliated. The twins grew to despise each other so much that they no longer had parties, nor did they attend anymore public events. You dudes follow me?" asked Harlo.

They nodded intensely, waiting for the rest of the story.

"Anyway, these twins, who were older, were still fighting all the time. Until one day on their 17th birthday, when it came time for them to marry, they began to battle over the same woman. They started screaming and yelling at each other in the ballroom. Addison was so mad he drew his sword. Just as he was about to fight his brother, his mother bounded into the room, startling Addison, who turned and accidentally struck his mother with the sword! Horrified and angered at what Addison had done, Alistair drew his sword and just as Addison went to help his mother he slipped in the blood and impaled himself on his own sword that had stabbed his mother! His father, upon hearing the screaming, charged into the ballroom to see the gruesome scene.

The Duke immediately fought with Alistair; thinking that he had murdered the Duchess and Addison, not knowing what had actually happened. The father and Alistair struggled while Alistair tried to explain what had happened, but it was too late. It is said that while the Duke tried to subdue Alistair, he wrestled his sword away, and accidentally killed him with his sword…at the exact moment that Alistair yelled that his brother Addison had killed his mother, not him!" said Harlo with a shudder.

"So, dude, what happened to the dad?" asked Terrence.

"Well, that's what nobody knows. The story goes that he tried to save Alistair, but it was too late. So, totally freaked out and in despair, he vanished. Never to be seen again."

"No kidding? That's it? He just disappeared?" asked Pal, upset.

"That's crude!" said Donell trying to shake it off.

"So, nobody knows what happened to the Duke?" asked Terrence.

"Nobody knows for sure. They say the servants came running in to the ballroom and saw the horrible scene, but he was nowhere to be found, gone, vanished…Some stories say that in his despair he rode his horse off a cliff behind the castle. The horse was found at the bottom of the cliff, but they never found the Duke's body. Some say he just disappeared, pouf! Either way he never came back."

"What happened to all his riches?" asked Terrence.

"Here's the other weird part. Weeks later, it came out that the dude was almost broke. He had lost his businesses and was shunned by everybody -- some say because he had his sons help him blackmail people -- others say because of the sons' fighting, people started to shun them."

"And your friend, GT, told you this whole story?" questioned Pal.

Harlo nodded.

"So, then what happened to the castle?" asked Pal.

"It became haunted! The servants fled that very same night, saying that the ghosts of the Duchess, Addison and Alistair roamed the castle – wailing all night long!

As the years went by, countless wealthy people and nobility bought the castle – over and over again, and tried to live in it. People even had it wired with electricity and modernized up to 100 years ago. That's when it was finally left for good! It's so haunted by the terrorizing, enraged spirits that nobody can stay there for even one night!

People have been pushed out of windows, locked in closets, the lights go on and off, water floods the place, stuff falls, tons of freaky stuff happens. The theory is that the mother and the two sons angrily haunt the castle, looking for the Duke. Until they are united, their souls cannot rest." Harlo finished the story while everyone sat silently.

They hadn't noticed that the cab driver had taken them a good distance outside of London. They had past by several small towns, the last one – Twickenshire. In fact they hadn't even seen the villagers a few miles back staring

128

intently at the cab, as they drove past heading up Brogden Street toward the castle.

BRRRRIIINNNGGG, BRRRRIIINGGG!

"What's that?" Pal jumped.

"Relax, dude, it's Harlo's phone," said Donell.

Harlo pulled his phone out of his pocket to see that it was Ira. One by one their phones rang, but they ignored them. They were too stunned with the castle story to bother with Ira.

Seconds later, looming in front of them, high atop a hill was the most wicked looking castle they had ever seen!

"There it is! Stop the cab!" yelled Harlo.

The cabdriver slammed the car to a dead stop startling them when he began to yell, "Everybody, bloody aut! RIGHT NOW! Forget the fair, joost git aut! Had I known ye were comin' ere to this place, I would've never taken yer fare!"

"But, how…how will we get back?" stammered Pal.

"Take a card! Call the company. They'll send somebody!" He threw a business card into the back seat, Terrence picked it up. When they were barely out of the cab, the driver gunned the engine and took off. Dust filled the air as the cab flew down the road while the back doors flapped shut.

"You'd think he saw a ghost, or something. Heh…heh!" Pal faked laughter.

"Yeah, but now we're stuck in the middle of nowhere," snapped Donell at Harlo, "and this place doesn't look too friendly."

"Well, at least Ira won't bother us," said Terrence.

They happily agreed as they slowly moved toward an opening in the dilapidated, low stone wall at the bottom of the hill.

Thirty-three
The Castle Cloon de Sade

It looked like there were tire marks leading up the hill to the castle, which they thought seemed odd. They began trudging up the hill, following the path. They were glad to find that the overgrown bramble and weeds had been flattened. As they made their way closer to the castle, it seemed like the skies were growing darker.

"Okay, if there's any lightening, I am so outta here!" whined Pal.

"That's only in the movies dude," said Terrence.

Seconds later, lightening crackled in the sky directly above the castle.

They looked at each other with eyes widening and began running up the hill.

The castle sat at the very top of the hill. At the entrance was an enormous stone gatehouse ravaged by hundreds of years of wear and tear. They entered the large archway and stopped to catch their breath.

"Man, that dude had some coin!" said Donell standing in front of the immense castle.

They cautiously climbed the giant stone steps leading up to the gigantic castle doors. The size of everything was mind boggling. Even the evil looking chipped old gargoyles guarding what once represented enormous wealth and success were huge. There were numerous tall towers with tarnished pointed metal spires high above them. A rusty old gate creaked in the wind.

They approached the mammoth door made of heavy wood with big black bolts and crusty metal strips. Harlo reached for the gigantic door knocker. It was a gargoyle's face partially covered with green moss and rust.

The thuds echoed loudly through the building, sounding hallow.

"What do you think the ghosts are gonna do? Open the door and say, c'mon in, glad you're here!" joked Donell.

"Looks like nobody's home, so...let's head back!" shivered Pal.

Harlo and Terrence began to push on the gigantic door, but it wouldn't budge.

"Hey, my friend, GT, told me to go around to the right side. There's a small opening that we can get in through," instructed Harlo. They moved down the steps, around to the side of the massive castle.

"So, what exactly is your friend's name again?" asked Terrence.

"GT," mumbled Harlo.

"Oh, GT, and what does that stand for?"

"Ghost Talker."

They glanced at each other as they walked along the side of the castle.

"There it is!" yelled Harlo. He pointed to a small opening on the side of the castle. Three large stones had been moved from the castle wall.

"Well, you go first," said Donell to Harlo.

"Okay, no problemo," Harlo got on the ground, while holding his laptop on his stomach with one hand, he began to scoot his legs through.

"AAAAAGGGGGHHHH!" Harlo screamed at the top of his lungs!

Donell jumped into Pal's arms.

"WHAAATTT? What's wrong?" Terrence yelled.

Harlo's eyes widened and he froze staring straight up.

"Oh no! He's dead! He's dead! They must've cut off his legs!" screamed Pal at the top of his lungs as he dropped Donell on the ground. Pal covered his eyes and began running around in circles.

Harlo blinked his eyes numerous times, "Just kidding!" he said cracking up while laying on the ground halfway through the opening.

"You jerk!" screamed Donell.

Terrence had to hold Donell back. Harlo immediately stopped laughing and scooted as fast as he could through the small opening in to the castle.

"Okay…your turn," said Terrence to Pal, as Pal began to regain his composure.

Pal shook his head 'NO.' Terrence shook his head at the nonsense of it all, got on the ground and shimmied himself through the opening into the fearsome castle.

Not wanting to stay outside, Donell quickly followed. When it was Pal's turn, he got stuck halfway through and they had to yank him in.

Thirty-four
Inside the Haunted Walls

Once inside the dark, dank castle they were astonished. The opening had led into the foyer which was gigantic. There were several different huge, arched stone doorways all around the entryway. There was a light switch on the wall. Terrence went and flicked it, nothing happened.

Where there weren't doorways, there were stone cut-outs with ancient armor standing in them. There were sets of swords and axes displayed on the walls centered around the Cloon de Sade coat of arms.

Two massive carved wooden staircases led up either side of the gigantic foyer. On the side of the front door there was a smaller staircase winding up to a tower.

There was a large, ornate crystal chandelier lined with thousands of tiny dusty light bulbs in the center of the room. Exquisite old tapestries covered the walls, and faded velvet curtains with dingy gold tassels were everywhere, clinging to diamond paned windows and decorating the passageways into other rooms. There was dusty, oversized, carved wood furniture – chairs, desks and tables lining the walls. Huge, fancy candelabras with half-melted candles in them and metal cups and plates were scattered about. It was like an abandoned museum, decrepit with heavy dust and cobwebs everywhere.

"Wow, I can't believe that a place like this just sits here empty," said Pal.

"Where I come from, if a place is left empty too long, people break in and even take the copper pipes," said Donell quietly as he looked around.

"Where I come from, our pipes are plastic," added Terrence.

"Let's check out the rest of this place," said Harlo.

"Uh…yeah, and fast. You know before it gets dark out. We won't be able to see where we're going. And uh…I think we should stick together," continued Pal.

They moved slowly and cautiously from room to room in complete awe of the gigantic, undisturbed castle.

"Man this thing is as big as me!" said Donell standing in a fireplace that was taller than him, and four times as wide.

"Do be a good chap and bring me my brandy in the drawing room…" said Harlo as he sat down on an old, dusty wooden chair with torn velvet covering.

"CAAAWWW, CAAAWWW!!!"

Harlo covered his head and hit the floor as a blackbird dove through the room screeching. The bird found its way out of one of the small broken window panes and flew away.

"Yo, Harlo! King, dude, you sure you're up to this ghost hunting business?" asked Terrence as they laughed.

Down the hall through a smaller arched doorway was a drawing room. Sticking together, they walked across the creaking floor, back through the foyer and into a massive ballroom. The walls were lined in dusty gold trim with faded floral patterns painted on them. The entire ballroom floor was black and white checked marble tiles.

"This is where they say it happened," whispered Harlo, "the ballroom."

"No kidding…look, all those stones are brown!" pointed Terrence toward the middle of the room.

"Ouuuuuu, gross!" said Pal shielding his eyes. He stayed behind as the others went to take a closer look. It looked like what they thought it was; dried blood that had seeped into the porous holes of the white tile and discolored it forever. It was a grisly site!

"Hey! Look at those pictures!" said Pal. There were huge dusty portraits that hung crookedly on the walls.

In the middle was one massive portrait with four people.

"Harlo, I think we found your family," said Terrence.

"Harlo joined them and slowly read the scrawled metal plate below the dusty framed portrait, "Duke Gregario

Cloon de Sade, Duchess Margola Wharton Cloon de Sade, Addison & Alistair Cloon de Sade. Hmmm…"

A chill ran up and down his spine. They stood frozen looking at the portrait. It was almost as if you could tell that the faces of the Duke and Duchess were sad as they looked toward their two sons. Both boys were dressed identical, and were staring at each other with contempt and hatred.

"Okay, I feel bad for the Cloon de Sades, but worse for my stomach. It's growlin', bros, and we got a long way back. So, let's find these poltergeists and then go get some dinner. Plus, it's getting really cold in here," pleaded Pal as he shook off the chill that he felt.

"C'mon, dudes…" said Harlo, disappointed.

"Hey! We came all the way out here. We gotta at least let Harlo see the place. What if we board?" asked Donell.

"Through the castle?" questioned Harlo.

"Gnarly idea! We'll get through it faster and get some practice in!" agreed Terrence excitedly.

They strapped on their helmets, jumped on their boards and began flying through the castle. It was the perfect place to board. Grinding anything with a ledge, they pumped through the halls and archways. They ollied up on top of old desks and across the enormous dining room table, then kick flipped and rode down flights of stairs doing hand Caspers.

"Bro, you're a natural!" Pal said to Donell.

"And you're a ripper!" laughed Donell.

It was the first time they really freestyled together. They realized that they had a similar style – something different from other boarders. They all did variations of the Casper tricks, which they found strange since they were in a supposedly haunted castle. They were fluid and smooth. It must've had something to with why they had been chosen as the contest winners.

"Dudes, I say we check out the upstairs, then grind some rails back down!" said Terrence.

They ran up the stairs and boarded down the long dark hallways. They were kick flipping through old bedrooms and around corners. They would jump across beds as the boards rolled under them and met them at the other side.

They had forgotten all about being in a haunted castle as their wheels sped across the old floors. The more they boarded the colder the castle seemed to get. With the echoing sound and vibration of their wheels they didn't notice the disturbance that was going on in the castle.

They rounded back through the massive hallways to the top of the stairs.

"Did you hear that?" asked Harlo stopping.

"I didn't hear anything except wheels in motion!" said Donell.

"Look, mates, I think we could go for days and not see this entire castle, I say there's no spirits and we gotta get back," said Terrence.

"Yeah, I agree," nodded Donell, out of breath.

"Oooouuuuu… Ira is gonna be furious that we didn't stay with our cultural tour!" said Pal in a funny impression of Ira.

Harlo nodded as they finished by grinding down either side of the massive staircase railings.

They found the small spot they had crawled in through, and scooted back out. It took all three of them to replace the heavy stones.

Thirty-five
The Twickenshire Pub

Luckily they had found their way back to the small village of Twickenshire. They had tried to use their quad phones near the castle, but ironically the phones were dead. They thought it was weird since they were supposed to work anywhere in the world. But they hadn't been able to pick up a signal until they crossed the village line.

It would take at least 40 minutes to get a cab out to them the dispatcher told Terrence. So they found a local pub and went inside for a beverage while they waited.

"No ghosts in that castle, dude," said Terrence shaking his head.

"Yeah, and our awesome Caspers would certainly wake the dead," said Pal. "Look, bros, I believe in spirits. I could tell you some scary stories about Hawaii..."

They proceeded chatting about spirits while their iced tea was delivered. The waitress couldn't help but overhear them.

"Don't go back," she said sternly, yet quietly in her English accent.

"Excuse me?" said Terrence as they stopped talking and stared at her.

141

"Don't go back. I mean, if you're talking about Castle Cloon De Sade…" she whispered with a terrified look in her eye. She bent down next to the round wooden table and quietly introduced herself as Emily.

She began to tell them some of the horrors of what had just happened to the Ghost Hunters. How they were in the hospital and just coming out of shock. She told them about the terrifying stories through the years… but was suddenly interrupted by her boss.

"Emily, I need your assistance!" A man shouted.

She quickly walked away as they overheard him say, "What did I tell you about talkin' to patrons concerning the castle? C'mon, Em,…you can't scare away our business."

"Ouuuu, she's a Betty!" said Pal, stretching his neck to watch her.

"Dude, you're a hound! Are there any girls you aren't attracted to?" asked Donell.

"Well, my family," said Pal.

"You're gross!" laughed Donell.

The cab pulled up in front of the small pub and they left. Harlo was quiet after what Emily had said.

When they started to leave, he turned back to look at the pub owner who was watching their every move. Harlo awkwardly waved goodbye while walking backwards out of the pub. Emily peeked out the kitchen door, while shaking her head 'no' to Harlo from behind the man.

Weird! He thought to himself, but knew that Ghost Talker was right. If the village people believed in the ghosts, then it had to be true. He was going to have to find out for himself.

Thirty-six
A Grievance

Once they got back to the hotel, they found angry notes taped to their hotel room doors. Ira was furious. If they didn't show up by 6:00 pm on the dot they were off the tour! That gave them exactly three minutes to get back downstairs. They tore out of their rooms and down the stairs.

Ira was standing in the lobby looking at his watch angrily while Brie paced anxiously.

"Lucky you made it! Where the hell have you been?" He yelled.

They followed him to a secluded area of the lobby and grabbed a seat.

"In lieu of your recent actions, I have had Cheese here file a formal grievance in regards to your staying on this tour," stated Ira.

"What? C'mon, man! You can't do that!" they all objected.

"I can and I did. I cannot be responsible for your actions, or for your well being when you vanish into thin air!" Ira continued.

Every chance Brie got she would try to shoot them a look, letting them know that Ira was bluffing. Brie gave

Harlo a quick wink and he knew. *Whew.* Harlo thought to himself, knowing that she hadn't filed a grievance.

"…and if you ever leave from where you are supposed to be again, I will make sure you are replaced in an instant. Like that!" Ira said snapping his fingers in Donell's face. "You morons! Why do you think they have second runners up?!! You are free to have dinner. Cheese will make sure you're taken care of."

At dinner, Brie explained why she didn't make the call. Ira really didn't have any pull in the company, so she wasn't afraid of him. In fact, this was his last chance to prove himself. He knew if he had any problems on this tour – it would reflect on his lack of management, bad people skills and arrogance. He couldn't afford to raise eyebrows. But they still had to be careful, because he was known to have a temper and if pushed too far, he just might make the call.

"I knew it!" said Donell.

"Yeah, so did I!" said Terrence.

"He could care less about our well being. He is just one of those fat cats that uses everybody. I don't know why he can't just be nice!" said Ming in her normal voice.

Everyone at the table became silent. When Ming realized what she had done, she started to cough, explaining that she had a frog in her throat.

"It was this tour for Ira, or they were going to lay him off from the company!" Brie stated loudly, hoping to distract the attention away from her friend Ming.

Brie was determined to help Ming keep her secret so she could get a new agent. And Ming promised Brie that she would keep tabs on the guys, to help Brie move ahead in her new career and get a new boss.

Harlo was having fun and didn't want to leave the group. But there was a gnawing feeling in the pit of his stomach, and it wasn't hunger. He decided he would have to go back to the castle by himself. *What could possibly happen?* He stood up and announced that he wasn't feeling well. He was going to get some sleep in order to be ready for the big kickoff tomorrow.

Brie said she understood, while the rest of the guys looked at him suspiciously.

"I think he's just bummed that he didn't find his ghosts," said Pal.

"What?" asked Brie surprised.

Pal scrambled to make up a senseless story as they all began to talk at once, quickly changing the conversation back to Ira, and what they could do to put up with him during the tour. Brie told them that they would have to be careful; Ira had gotten the keys to their rooms and was planning on doing surprise checks on them.

Thirty-seven
Harlo's Dead

After dinner they headed back to their rooms deciding to get some sleep in order to be ready for the big day.

When Pal got to his room, he saw Harlo was already in bed. He tried chatting with him, but Harlo was asleep. Pal put the television on low and clicked to a sports station.

On TV there happened to be a World Cup skateboarding competition. Pal decided this was something Harlo wouldn't want to miss.

"Bro! Hey, bro! You gotta check this out! This dude is tight! Man he just backflipped!"

But there was silence from Harlo's side of the room.

"Seriously, he did it over an alligator pit and he was on a mountain board! No joke!" laughed Pal.

But there was no response from Harlo. His covered body was perfectly still.

"Harlo?"

Pal slowly got out of bed, moved over to Harlo's bed and poked him.

"Ohhhhh, no…not me! Please wake up, Harlo," Pal said louder, poking him again.

But still nothing! Pal tried again and when Harlo didn't move Pal screamed and tore out of the room. He ran across the hall and pounded on the door.

"Donell! Bro! It's me Pal, open up!"

"What? What is it?" asked Donell as he sleepily opened the door.

"Dude…Dude, Harlo's…" and Pal made a motion with his finger across his throat.

"What in the world are you talking about?" asked Donell confused.

"Harlo's dead!" cried Pal now pulling Donell by the arm across the hall.

"Don't touch me!" snapped Donell who was crabby from being woken up.

"Oh, sorry, man…" said Pal, patting Donell on the arm where he had pulled him. Donell slapped Pal's hand.

"Go ahead, see for yourself! I knew he shouldn't fool around with that paranormal stuff…I just knew it!" Pal pointed hysterically to the still figure on the bed and covered his eyes.

"Oh yeah, he's dead alright!" said Donell laughing as he pulled the covers back. Pal slid open two of his fingers that were covering his eyes to peek at the four pillows laying in a row.

"What the he…?" questioned Pal.

Harlo was gone! They knew the only place he would've gone alone without telling them was back to the creepy old castle. They didn't know what to do and decided they better get Terrence, without letting Ming know.

Donell dialed Terrence's room. When Ming answered Donell shoved the phone at Pal as he disguised his voice in his best English accent.

"One second," said Ming as she handed the phone to Terrence.

"Uh-huh, uh-huh," said Terrence into the phone, trying not to look surprised. He hung up and turned to look at Ming who was wrapped up in blankets like he was in the North Pole with his hat on.

"I have a package at the front desk," whispered Terrence quietly, grabbing his clothes, helmet and board as he tiptoed out of the room.

Pal's door was open as he let himself in.

"You can't be serious!" said Terrence breaking out in laughter.

"This is not a time to laugh!" said Pal.

"Not about Harlo, it's your little skateboard jammies!" Terrence continued laughing.

"Leave my pajamas out of this, my mother made them for me!" scolded Pal.

They knew Harlo had gone back to the castle. He was much braver that they would have ever given him credit

149

for. It was already 9:00 at night. They were afraid to go back themselves. Nevertheless, they knew they had to find Harlo.

Thirty-eight
Riding Horses

They got dressed and snuck out of the hotel's back exit, away from the busy street. They crept down the dark alleyway until they were a good distance from the hotel, then hailed a cab.

When they told the cabbie where they needed to go, he barked, "Bloody American's shoot me door!" and sped away without them.

"Shoot his door? Now that would be a silly thing to do!" joked Pal.

The next cab driver that pulled up was only told they were going to the village of Twickenshire. Donell dozed off on the way, while Pal kept asking Terrence 'What ifs?' about Harlo.

"What if he's not there? What if he's kidnapped? What if there really are ghosts? What if we can't get back in? What if I get hungry?"

Terrence, normally a very patient person, finally lost it and told Pal to put a lid on it.

The driver pulled into the small square in the center of Twickenshire. Terrence asked him if he could take them a tiny bit further like to the Castle Cloon de Sade. The cabbie shook his head vehemently saying, "Absolutely not."

They paid the driver and began to make their way through the tiny village toward the road to the castle. When they walked past the pub, the girl that had waited on them was closing and sweeping up.

"Hey, it's you! Uhh…Em," said Pal.

"Emily, and nice to see you again!" she said. "Are you staying at the lodge in the village?"

"Uh, no…no. Do you remember our bro who was into ghosts?" asked Pal as he began to explain what they were doing there.

Her face went pale. She whispered for them to meet her behind the pub.

They found their way to the back of the building, only to find her walking toward them with two horses. She said to take the horses, that if they didn't get back to the castle quickly they may never see their friend again. Emily instructed them that once they got to the bottom of the castle hill to leave the horses there, and not to take them any closer. Until *hopefully*, they made it back alive.

"Hopefully?!" questioned Pal surprised.

"Forget hopefully! Ride a horse? Ya'all are crazy! I ain't never rode no horse!" exclaimed Donell.

"Then ride with me. I do it every day at the ranch. It's part of my job," said Terrence as he jumped on, then

152

held out his arm to help Donell up. He shakily pulled Donell up. Donell managed to get settled on the horse begrudgingly, then quickly wrapped his arms around Terrence's waist as if his life depended on it.

"Don't go gettin' no ideas, California boy!" whined Donell as Terrence chuckled.

"Nice horsey…nice horsey…" said Pal as he unsteadily climbed up on the other horse.

"Giddy-yup!" snapped Terrence and his horse took off.

"Yeah, giddy-yup!" copied Pal. But his horse didn't move until Emily smacked the horse on its behind, giving it a good, "Hiya!" and the horse took off full steam.

"Okay, yeah…Hiya! Or it could be Hi ya? Like hi ya horsey, how yaaaaa doinnnn?" Pal yelled nervously.

"They're good mares, as long as you don't try to take them past the wall, you'll be fine!" Emily shouted. "Hopefully, I'll see you again!"

"Okay, like I am sick of that hopefully woooorrrrddd…." yelled Pal galloping off into the darkness.

When they were within a close enough distance to the castle, they stopped the horses, hopped off, and began walking. When they got too close, the horses began to get skittish, pulling back so they tied them up to a tree.

"Now, wait there, little horsey…good horsey," said Pal.

"Look, dude! There's a light on in the castle!" exclaimed Terrence.

"No kidding! Told you fools there's no such thing as ghosts…Harlo's just messin' with us!" said Donell, as they began once again to make their way up the flattened path.

Luckily, they had found a big flashlight in the maid's supply closet before they left the hotel. Because even though there was a light on in the castle, the only thing that lit the castle grounds was the eerie glow from the full moon. Now a dense fog was beginning to settle in and cover the land.

Thirty-nine
Finding Harlo

When they made it to the gate, the lights inside the castle blinked off.

"Okay, what is Harlo trying to pull here?" insisted Terrence.

"Whatever it is, it's not funny! I need my beauty sleep for tomorrow," whined Pal.

Once again, they tried the front door, but it still wouldn't budge. They carefully used the huge iron gargoyle knocker, and after a few minutes of waiting, they decided to try the opening in the wall again. The minute they walked down the steps, the enormous door slowly creaked open.

"Oh, you're hilarious Harlo! What'd you and Ira get together and plan this?" yelled Terrence. There was no reply.

"Harrrrlllllooo, oh Harrrlllooooo," Donell sang out.

But still no answer.

"Okay then. He's not here…let's go," said Pal sheepishly, turning around.

"Then who opened the door?" asked Terrence as he grabbed Pal's shirt from the back. "C'mon, you guys can hang out here if you want, but I'm goin' in."

"Me, too!" said Donell.

"Who can argue with that?" agreed Pal as he quickly squeezed in between Donell and Terrence.

Terrence held the flashlight steady as they moved into the castle. Inside it was pitch black and a whole lot creepier in the dark. They walked in slowly, within seconds the chandelier in the foyer came on!

"Okay, either Harlo is playing some really nasty joke, or there is a short in that thing!" said Donell.

"Yeah, but who's payin' the electric bill?" asked Terrence, "I know from experience that if nobody pays the bill then you don't get power – short or no short!"

Donell and Pal glanced at Terrence knowing he must've had a hard life.

BAM!!!

"What was that?" whispered Pal.

"It sounded like a door slamming. I think it came from up there," said Donell.

They dashed up the stairs and went room to room.

"Harlo! Dude! C'mon, enough with the games…Our tour kicks off tomorrow and you're our teammate! We need you, dude!" stated Terrence.

"Yeah! We can't be playin' pansy games in some nasty old castle!" agreed Donell.

The lights went out again.

"What if it's…it's not Harlo?" whispered Pal.

"Then, I don't know," Terrence replied quietly.

156

"Heh, heh, heh…yeah, like Harlo is probably back in the cozy hotel room sleeping by now," added Pal.

They continued creeping down the hall.

"AAAAGGGGGGHHHHH!!!" A hideous scream echoed through the castle!

"What the?" shuddered Donell.

They ran back downstairs, sticking together, to where it sounded like the horrible sound had come from. Moonlight was shining in through the windows as a shadowy figure glided across the floor and quickly out of the room through another doorway!

"Did you see that?" Donell asked.

"Yeah! Harlo!" yelled Terrence as they took off following the figure!

They ran through hallways as swinging doors would fly open and shut. They could hear footsteps ahead of them, as they followed the sounds down dark corridors, past creepy rooms. When they got to a huge old kitchen the footsteps stopped. Candles were burning, lighting up the room.

The three of them froze in the doorway.

"What the heck?" asked Donell, "Man, I like the dude and everything but he's starting to creep me out!"

A strong gust of cold air went through the room and the candles flickered. Again, the shadow darted through the room as the three began to chase after it! When they turned another corner they were back in the ballroom.

"EEEEEEYYYYYYAAAAAOUUUUU!!!!"
screamed Pal at the top of his lungs as he pointed at a wall
that was now dripping in blood! Pal turned and ran out of
the room as fast as he could!

Terrence and Donell stared in shock as blood poured
down the wall. They quickly turned and ran after Pal! Pal
had made it to the front door which was now closed!

"Mama!" yelled Pal pounding on the front door
while pulling on the knob trying to get it open. But it
wouldn't budge! Candles now lit up the foyer. Terrence and
Donell ran up to Pal, and when they patted him on the back
he almost jumped out of his skin!

"I wanna go home!" screamed Pal at the top of his
lungs, rushing to find the moveable stones. Pal kicked and
pushed on every stone, but not one of them would budge!

"Pal, you gotta calm down, dude!" Donell yelled at
the top of his lungs, shocking Pal.

"Okay, I'm okay, okay and you guys are
okay…everything is okay…EXCEPT WE CAN'T GET
OUT OF THIS FREAKIN' PLACE!!!" Pal bellowed.

"Of course we can…" said Terrence calmly, pushing
Pal away from the wall while trying to find the stones
himself. Not one would move!

Donell tried the door. Pal was right. The door
wouldn't open either.

"Look, I know for a fact that Ira is behind this!" said Donell.

"Really?" asked Pal calming down a bit.

"Yeah, sure. No doubt, dude," Donell tried to act sure of himself for Pal's sake, even though he wasn't.

"Okay, if Ira is behind this, then what is that?" asked Pal as he pointed to billowing curtains leading to another room!

"They got some kick butt special effects in here, that's all," said Terrence as he walked over to the curtains. They instantly stopped moving. He looked around for a fan, a vent, or a string or something that could've made them move.

He peered into a nearby room where a lit lantern flickered in the darkness barely lighting the room. Donell and Pal followed closely behind Terrence. Out of the corner of his eye Terrence saw something halfway under a chair.

He slowly turned to look. It was Harlo's computer and skateboard!

"No way, dude! Harlo would never let those things get out of his hands! They're far too precious to him! Something's really, really wrong here!" exclaimed Pal. Pal was now much calmer when he realized that his friend Harlo was in serious trouble.

Seconds later the chandelier, the candles, and the lantern went out.

Forty
The Evil Twins

The three shuddered as they stood in total darkness. Terrence turned on the flashlight, then picked up Harlo's computer. He unzipped the computer case and opened the laptop. It instantly clicked on to instant message.

"There can't be wireless way out here. We can't even get phone reception," said Donell.

Slowly, letter by letter, a message filled the screen.

'You only have a brief amount of time to save your friend, Harlo. Go release them...Find the missing Duke and the third s...'

The screen went black as the computer went dead.

"What's that supposed to mean?" asked Pal.

Terrence quickly closed the laptop and put it in the bag. Pal grabbed Harlo's skateboard and helmet.

"AAAAAGGGGHHHHHH!!!" Another wail shattered the silence. The candles instantly re-lit themselves, then out of nowhere two freakish-looking men stood in the entrance to the room!

Terrence, Donell and Pal froze as their mouths dropped open.

It was the twins! They were hideous looking! They were medium height and slender, with angular looking angry faces and pitch black hair pulled into a pony tail. They wore tattered long red jackets with tarnished gold buttons and black trim. Their white shirts were ripped and dirty with dusty black breeches, torn socks and dusty black, high shoes. But the most horrible part of all was the splattered blood stains with huge gaping, bloody holes in each of them!

"It's the dudes from the portraits!" choked Pal.

The second the twins heard Pal speak, they stiffly began to move their way!

"Ride!" screamed Terrence as he whipped Harlo's laptop over his shoulder.

They jumped on their boards and pushed off as they lunged down the curving narrow hallway as fast as they could. They were riding fast and smooth as they went up and over a couch! They power slid into a sitting area and ducked behind an enormous old carved desk for a second.

"We can't out-skate ghosts!" said Donell trying to catch his breath.

"We can try!" said Terrence.

"I think I'm gonna be ill!" cried Pal.

"Just ride!" yelled Terrence.

They ducked into a library and stood breathlessly as they looked around.

161

Moments later a gigantic bookshelf started shaking behind them. Hundreds of huge old leather bound books began to fall on their heads! They quickly moved out of the way, but just as they did, the two identical men appeared right in front of them!

"Here! Catch!" yelled Donell as he heaved one of the heavy books at the twins. It caught the twins completely off guard as they went to catch it and tumbled backwards awkwardly.

It gave the three of them just enough time to get back on their boards and speed out of the double doors of the library and back down the long hallway! They moved toward the foyer using the wall going upstairs as a launch ramp. They were out-skating ghosts!

Once they got to the top of the stairs they ripped down another hall. They flew past doors that were opening and slamming shut! They were ducking portraits that were flying off the walls and just missing vases that were being hurled at them from out of nowhere! When they had almost made it to the last door at the end of the hallway, it slammed shut, right on Donell! But when the front of his skateboard accidentally banged into the closed door, a hidden passageway next to it immediately slid open.

"Look! In there!" yelled Pal.

"I don't know…" said Donell.

"Get in, we don't have a choice!" exclaimed Terrence.

They quickly climbed through the opening and began tapping and pushing on the wall to close the secret panel. Luckily, it slid shut! They looked around the tiny space while trying to catch their breath and listening for the hideous twins. Terrence shined the flashlight around the small enclosed area; they could see they were standing in some kind of secret, old cage-like pulley in a mysterious stone passageway.

"I think I know what they want!" Terrence whispered fiercely.

"What?" asked Donell.

"They want us to go back to the ballroom!"

"How do you know that? What are you? A ghostbuster or something?" questioned Pal.

"No, it's just a hunch…The murder happened in the ballroom, right?"

Donell and Pal nodded as Terrence continued to explain his theory, based on what he had gotten from Harlo and GT.

"…they have a reason for roaming the castle. They need to be set free. They need mortals to help them solve or find something. They keep trying to re-enact the murder – over and over again.

"With us?" questioned Pal his face filled with fear.

"I'm not sure, but either way we need to stay away from that ballroom! I have a feeling if we find Harlo, we might be able to figure out what really happened to the Cloon de Sades."

"And if we can't, then what?" insisted Donell.

"Well, I don't want to find out," said Pal.

"This has to lead to somewhere! C'mon!" said Terrence as he shined the flashlight around the eerie passage.

The light of the flashlight shined on a rope that was tied to a giant wooden bracket in the stone. They carefully untied the rope while holding onto it.

"Be careful, this thing is ancient," said Donell.

Together, they gradually began lowering themselves down.

They clung to the rope, while the ancient pulley would creak as the metal cage swayed.

"I just hope this thing can hold my lard butt," said Pal, "I doubt that it's made as strong as our boards!"

"Look, what's that?" asked Donell as the flashlight illuminated the stone wall.

Donell took the flashlight and shined it on two dust-covered canvas and wood flaps. While Pal and Terrence held the rope tightly, Donell leaned out of the pulley and moved the flaps.

"It's a spy hole! It looks right into the ballroom!"

"Over there!" said Terrence.

164

Just a few feet away was a big stone ledge. They swung the small cage over to the ledge to rest while tightening the rope. Next to the ledge was another secret panel. Once they were secured, Terrence carefully slid the warped panel open. The small door lead right into the ballroom! Terrence quickly slid it shut again.

"It's the ballroom alright!" whispered Terrence, "I don't want to take a chance!"

"Okay, back up we go," said Donell as they began to pull themselves back up, which was a lot harder than lowering themselves.

They went past the floor they had come from, and continued pulling the small cage they were in up to a higher level. Once there they found another ledge and panel. They quietly slid the panel open revealing another long, eerie dark dusty hallway. Only this hallway was small compared to the rest of the castle, and it was unfinished with no carpets or furniture. It had one small dusty round window high up at the far side. They silently crawled out through massive cobwebs. Mice would run squeaking by as giant spiders scurried about on their webs.

"Not diggin' this at all…No sir," moaned Pal.

Terrence shined the flashlight along the dusty stone floor, when something caught his eye.

"What is that?" asked Terrence, kneeling down. They moved in to take a closer look. It was more blood!

165

Forty-one
The Duchess

"Eeeyyoooouuuu, how could that have gotten here? And what's up with these secret passageways?" asked Pal.

They followed the old path of dried blood down the spine-chilling hallway. It led to another mysterious door.

Pal and Donell nodded at Terrence as he carefully slid it open.

Terrence shined the flashlight on what looked like old fabric. He carefully moved it to the side and they crawled through. Once inside, they realized they were in a huge closet. It was filled with dusty clothes. There were dozens of ancient faded Victorian gowns, hundreds of pairs of shoes with weird buckles and bows, and big dusty, curly wigs lined a shelf.

"Somebody forgot their clothes," whispered Donell, trying not to choke from the dust.

"There has to be another door," said Terrence, as he stood up.

"ere it isss," mumbled Pal, while trying to shield his mouth from the dust.

They slowly opened it and could see that it led into a spectacular bedroom. It had high, ornate ceilings and paintings of cupids covering the walls. Thick cobwebs and dust concealed heavy brocade bedding on a gigantic canopy bed. Tall curtains were pulled back to reveal a big paned window overlooking a cliff. Huge old dressers were ornately designed with curving lines and gold paint.

"Uhhh, did you dudes happen to notice that the lights are on in here?" asked Donell.

"Oh yeah, uh-huh. I noticed. But, like, I really didn't want to say anything," said Pal.

"Let's look around. There has to be some kind of clue in here…" said Terrence.

"You know, I was never any good at playing spy…I just want to find Harlo and get the heck out of here," said Pal nervously.

"Me, too, but there's more to this Cloon de Sade story than we know," said Terrence.

"Yeah, but what?" asked Donell, as he plopped down on the enormous bed and dust puffed out everywhere. He flagged away the dust while coughing, and when it had cleared, he looked at Pal and Terrence. He could see their faces had completely changed from somewhat scared to terrified as they stared at him. They tried to speak but could only point!

"What? Oh c'mon, not charades! Oh, okay, I'll play for a sec. I get it…you two look like you saw a ghost…am I right, huh, am I?" laughed Donell.

167

Pal and Terrence slowly nodded.

"Wait a minute, sounds like…" but within seconds, Donell had caught a glimpse in the mirror across the room.

Sitting up in the bed beside him was a ghastly figure of a Victorian woman! Her skin was blue-white and she had a massive bleeding hole in her chest. In a zombie-like trance she let out a hideous wail as blood ran down her chin! She suddenly reached her zombie hands out while grabbing Donell and trying to pull him toward her!

Pal and Terrence ran over and began to hit her with their skateboards. She released her grasp, but immediately jumped up and started to chase them! They ran out of the main bedroom door screaming!

Now they were in another hallway!

They jumped on their boards and grinded down the wooden rails to the next floor! They could hear her horrible screaming following them as they hit the next level and jumped off. They pushed as they zoomed back, trying to find the secret passageway. Once at the end of the hall, Donell jumped off his board again and slammed it into the wall!

The secret passageway slid open. As quickly as they could, they scrambled back into the metal cage and slammed the panel shut! Breathing heavily, they grabbed the rope and immediately began lowering themselves!

"Try that flippin' computer again dude!" said Pal shaking.

168

They finally reached the ballroom level. Once again, there was an uncanny silence, no screaming, no footsteps…just silence. Pal and Donell quietly tied the rope of the pulley to the bracket.

Terrence took the case off his back, unzipped it, and without even having to turn it on, the instant message came up!

'You know there is more than meets the eye. Harlo does, too. Find him before they find you! You have to know there is another… GT.'

The screen went black.

"Another? Another what?!" Terrence impatiently shook the computer.

"Don't break the thing. We need it, bro!" Pal insisted.

"Well, we can't go up and we don't want to stop at this floor. Let's see if this thing goes further down," said Donell. They untied the rope and found they could go lower than the main floor!

It seemed like they had lowered themselves pretty far down when the cage stopped. They hit the bottom! This time there was no sliding door…Terrence shined the flashlight around and they could see they were in a solid stone circular hole.

"Well, maybe there is another passageway somewhere," said Terrence, climbing out of the pulley. They began to feel the stones around the perimeter. They tried pushing on almost all of the large stones, but they wouldn't budge. They sat on the ground and began to use their feet as they pushed with all their might. Finally, one of the giant stones moved a bit. Seconds later, a huge secret door slowly began to open!

Forty-two
The Dungeon

They slowly moved into the pitch black darkness. Once inside the stale, musty-smelling room, Terrence shined the light around. They shuddered when they realized they were in a real dungeon!

"Oh my gosh!" said Terrence.

Pal moved closer to Terrence, "Uhhh, I'm not feeling so good."

Donell just swallowed.

"We'll be alright," said Terrence, wishing he could believe his own words.

The dungeon was a massive, horrible stone room. There was a steep stone staircase curving up one side of it leading to a heavy metal door. Scattered around the room were ancient rusty metal and wood torture devices.

They moved cautiously through the cobwebs and dust, not wanting to bump into anything while Terrence shined the flashlight around the gruesome place.

"Look! Torches!" said Donell.

Sticking together, they moved to get one. Terrence had a lighter. They kept their fingers crossed that the torch

would ignite. It flared up! They lit another one for Donell
as Pal tried to steady the flashlight in his shaking hands.

Now that they could see the evil room, they were
even more disgusted! Everywhere they looked there were
grisly torture mechanisms.

"Oh, dudes, this is far worse than the wax museum,
far worse! For some reason, I just didn't believe this kind of
stuff really existed!" moaned Pal.

There was a rack that was used to stretch people to
death, and huge compression units that crushed people.
Lining the walls were ropes for hanging, whips and blood-
stained daggers.

A pillory that was used to lock a person's head and
arms in, and lots of other horrible looking things – many
with blood stains and some with ancient looking bones in
them! "Oh no, please tell me those bones aren't real…pretty
please!" begged Pal.

Terrence and Donell shuddered, but were silent.

"Great, now I feel much better," said Pal.

As they slowly moved to the middle of the gruesome
torture equipment, there was a giant cauldron filled with foul
smelling, rotting oil.

"Uhh, I thought that the saying 'boiled in oil' was
just that – a saying…" shivered Donell.

"No, they really used to do that…I read about it
in…"

SQUEEEAAAKKK!!!

"OOOUUUUU!" They screamed as rats suddenly scampered around their feet. There were rats everywhere. Terrence and Donell shooed them away with the torches.

"I need a torch!" whined Pal. But just as he had spoken, another loud squeak came from above them.

"What was that?" asked Donell, "I hope it's not bats. Man, I hate bats. I can deal with rats, being from the city and all…but bats, uh-uh, no way!"

"Shhhhhh…listen…," said Terrence.

There was a creaking sound…then moaning!

They raised their torches, high above them they could see a grotesque human cage made of heavy metal strips in the shape of a human! Even more frightening there was someone in it!

The figure continued to groan.

"Not another ghost!" cried Pal.

"No, look! It's Harlo!" yelled Donell.

"It is! Hang loose Harlo…we'll get you down!" yelled Terrence.

They followed the line of the heavy thick rusted metal chain to an enormous circular wooden wheel mounted on the stone wall. Using all their strength, all three of them began to turn the wheel. Slowly, the heavy metal cage began to lower to the ground as Harlo groggily moaned.

"We're savin' you, bro, don't worry!" yelled Pal.

When the human cage finally reached the ground, Harlo began to wake up.

"Man, am I glad to see you guys…" Harlo mumbled. They pried open the heavy metal door and helped get him out.

"Are you okay, man?" questioned Donell.

"I think so. I don't know what happened…It was like the minute I got here I sat down at a desk in the library and opened up my computer…"

"So, how'd you end up down here?" asked Terrence.

"I don't know. All I remember is that I was bouncing my knee and I hit something under an old desk … some kinda secret compartment or something. Yeah, that's it…."

It was all coming back to Harlo now.

"When I bent down to look at what my knee hit, something bonked me on the head and I passed out! Look, bro, I know it sounds crazy. Maybe I ate some bad food," continued Harlo, as he rubbed his head.

"Oh, it's not crazy, believe me! And you sure didn't eat any bad food, dude…" said Pal, "I never heard of bad food locking you up in a human cage in the dungeon, man!"

"We should bonk you on the head for not telling us you were coming here!" said Terrence as they helped Harlo stand up.

174

"C'mon…right now we gotta get out of this evil place," said Donell.

As they began to make their way to the pulley, Terrence began to explain…

"When we got here, we found your computer. But it wasn't in the library…"

Harlo shook his head, "No?" inquisitively, and they shook their heads 'No' back.

"It was under a chair in that parlor area. We opened it up, and basically it said that in order for all of us to get out of here, we have to find the 'you know what' in this place. So, there is more to the creepy ghost stuff and this haunted castle than any of us know. Because who knows, what a you-know-what is?" as Terrence barely finished his sentence, it happened again…

"AAAGGGGHHHHHHHH!!!" another terrifying moan pierced the air.

"Quick! We've gotta move!" yelled Donell.

But it was too late.

Forty-three
A Ghostly Brawl

They didn't even make it near the secret passage when the grotesque figures of Addison and Alistair whipped down the stone stairs right toward them! This time they were both brandishing bloody swords! They stood ready to do battle as they moved in swiftly.

"Okay, you aren't kidding!" cried Harlo.

Instantly, Alistair swooped down toward Harlo swinging his sword. Harlo ducked and Alistair missed him by an inch, as his sword got stuck in the wooden pillory!

The hideous ghost wheeled back around grabbing Harlo by the hair. He began forcing Harlo's head and hands into the pillory! At that instant Pal screamed, "Heads up!" and threw Harlo's skateboard at the ghost hitting him right in head! The ghoul let go of Harlo as he spun around, allowing Harlo to grab his board and skate away on it.

For a split second, Alistair's head was gone, but then it popped back out! Now the twin was madder than ever!

They all began riding in circles around the twin poltergeists! Donell began to Monster Walk every time one of the ghosts would lunge toward him. They would jump over the ghosts, doing ollie impossibles and front foot impossibles. They would fly back and forth over and around the ghastly torture devices.

While Terrence blasted anti-caspers he grabbed onto a hangman's noose, swung from it and BAM! His skateboard hit Addison square in the face! The ghost spun around sending his sword flying away!

"GNARLY!" yelled Harlo, who was now back in full force.

But seconds later, the ghost brandished another weapon. This time, it was a stick with a ball and chain with huge metal spikes! The ghost swung it in circles over his head, gaining speed!

"Watch out!" screamed Terrence at the top of his lungs as they all boarded low, and hid behind the Iron Maiden. Just then, the ghost sent the grisly weapon flying through the air. It hit the metal human prison and clanged loudly!

"Okay, this could go on forever!" yelled Donell.

"Take this, you bonehead!" bellowed Pal as he pulled a can of Thrash Energy Drink from his pocket, did a complete uninhibited switch backside off the curving wall of the dungeon and dropped down right next to Alistair and sprayed the drink all over him!

The spirits began to seem woozy from watching them.

Pal was flying toward one of the ghosts when he began to wobble and missed! He headed straight for the heavy stone wall near the pulley!

"Pal, watch out!" hollered Donell. But it was too late! They covered their eyes -- not wanting to see their friend splat against the heavy stone wall!

Then, it happened! Even the evil twins froze when Pal hit the wall!

He hit it so hard that the stones gave way in a human shape as Pal rammed through it! But they weren't real stones! It was another phony concealed passageway!

"OOOUUUUUUWWWWW!!!" cried Pal, as he bumped, tumbled and fell into the dark hole. Suddenly, he stopped falling and there was silence for a second.

"EEEEYYYYOOOOUUU!!! Get me out of here! ANOTHER DEAD BODY!!!" Pal yelled at the top of his lungs!

Harlo, Donell and Terrence ran over to the dust-filled opening, waving away the rubble. Terrence tried to shine the torch down the dark narrow tunnel. They could barely see Pal! He was about twenty feet down trying desperately to back away from a skeleton that was buried up to his waist in dried mud!

"Heeeellllppp meeeee!" screamed Pal, as he cowered against the wall! The skeleton had long dirty matted black hair and a scruffy dried moustache on his bare bones; it was still wearing pieces of rotted clothes. There were scraps of old parchment paper lying around. A few feet away from it was an ancient half worn leather satchel. His skull was contorted with the look of horror, as if he had died with his mouth open screaming for help while struggling to get free. It was a repulsive site!

They suddenly realized they had forgotten about the ghosts and quickly looked around the dungeon, but the twins were gone!

Forty-four
The Last Ghost

"Please, please get me out of here!" cried Pal, while frantically trying to crawl back up out of the hole in the dust and dirt! But he would just slide back down toward the skeletal remains the more panicked he became.

Harlo quickly ran over and yanked on one of the old nooses that was dangling loosely on the side of the wall.

"Yuk!" he said as it fell into his hands.

He ran back to the opening and they quickly threw one end of the rope to Pal. They instructed him to hold on as tightly as he could. Pal managed to reach his board. He quickly tied the rope around it and then held onto it with all his might. Donell, Terrence and Harlo pulled as they helped get Pal out of the terrifying tunnel!

"Thanks for saving me, thanks so much, my bros. I love you guys!" cried Pal, while hugging them.

"Man, if I had to bet money on it I would say that dude is the old Duke!" said Pal, still somewhat hysterical while dusting himself off and pointing at the hole.

They agreed and figured that the Duke must've gotten trapped in muck and mud during his own secret escape! It was the Duke that the servants had heard wailing through the night!

BOOM! BOOM! BOOM!

Suddenly there were thunderous noises from above and another ear piercing wail as they looked around the dungeon.

Seconds later, a huge torrent of dust and sand began pouring out of the tunnel from where they had just rescued Pal! It was pouring right out of Cloon de Sade's death trap into the dungeon! The next instant, the entire castle began to rumble and shake!

"Let's get outta here!" said Terrence, tossing Harlo his computer. They ran up the stairs to the door that the twins had come from. But it was locked!

Sand was now filling the dungeon!

"To the pulley!" yelled Terrence as they darted back down the stairs shielding their faces with their boards.

They squeezed through the giant stone door that was now closing! They made it just in time!

181

They quickly crammed themselves into the pulley. Then, with all of their strength, they began pulling themselves up while avoiding pieces of falling rock and stones. The castle continued to shake!

Harlo quickly opened his computer while the others pulled.

It went right on again to GT... *"It's not a pleasant reunion they're after, but the end is near! Go to the library...let them relive the truth or you will all perish! GT."* He clicked off.

Harlo quickly typed in... "Dude, GT, we need your help! Perish? What are you saying?" But the screen instantly went black.

"Why does he talk like that? Like some kind of code..." asked Terrence anxiously while he continued pulling.

"Did he say anything else to you guys?" Harlo asked as he began to help pull.

"Yeah, but I can't remember. Wait, something about there being a third 'S'... What the heck does he mean by S?" asked Terrence.

They retraced the story comparing what Harlo knew, while trying to figure out what 'S' meant. The tried every word that they could think of that started with S...

"Song, sing, solo, shake, skin, scoop, skill, skateboard..."

"That's it! It's skateboard!" said Pal excitedly.

"How could it possibly be skateboard?" asked Donell.

"I don't know, because I like skateboards?" shrugged Pal.

"Okay, we are way off! Whatever it is that we need to find something that starts with S in order to get out of here! It has to have something to do with the murder." said Donell.

"Or maybe the weapon?" questioned Terrence.

"Oh yeah, you're good! That's it! Sword!!!" yelled Harlo, "There must be another sword! Maybe that's what's hidden in the library desk!"

They decided they had to get to the library as quick as possible to find out what was in the secret compartment of the desk.

This meant they were going to have to either go up to another level, up or go through the ballroom! They knew they didn't have time to waste! The castle was crumbling and shaking more than ever!

When they got to the ballroom level, they could hear moaning.

Donell secretly peered through the Duke's spy holes. Sure enough, all three ghosts were together in the ballroom!

"Dudes! It's so freaky! They are just floating around all bloody lookin' and moanin'! This crap is freakin' me out!" gagged Donell.

"It's okay, dude, but now what?" asked Harlo.

"We have no choice! We are just gonna have to ride through and fast. There is no time to waste!" said Terrence.

They readied their boards at the secret door, quickly counted to three, and slid open the panel. They pivoted out one by one, as fast as lightening. They skated through the ballroom and out the door to the foyer. They swooped down the hall toward the library.

The spirits were hot on their trail now! They ripped down the hallway, boarding so effortlessly that they looked like they were spirits themselves!

Suddenly, Addison caught up to Pal! He reached out his gruesome hand and yanked the back of Pal's ponytail! Pal quickly did a Late flip off nearby steps, looked at the ghost, lifted his arm and punched the ghost right in the face!

"Nobody messes with my hair!" Pal yelled as he turned back and quickly caught up with the team.

"Awesome!" yelled Terrence as they followed Harlo closely, then whipped around a dark corner into the library.

Once inside, they slammed the door and stood against it while trying to hold it closed. Harlo wallied over the huge desk. He caught his board, jumped down and

184

quickly crawled underneath the massive old thing and tapped along the panels.

"Better hurry up! And why are we holding this door? They can go through walls!" yelled Donell.

"I found it!" screamed Harlo.

As he jammed the hollow spot with his board, a door dropped open. An ancient sword caked with dried blood fell out.

"This is it! The missing sword!" yelled Harlo. He carefully held it up by his t-shirt without touching it. But seconds later, the three ghosts burst through the walls!

They froze when they saw Harlo holding the sword.

Eerily, they began to move toward him.

"Uhhh…I'm not so sure we want them to have that," said Terrence.

"It's part of what we've been looking for, for hundreds of years," a spooky echo of a voice came from the ghastly bluish Duchess.

"I think I should give it to them!" stated Harlo, his voice trembling.

He carefully placed the sword on the desk and backed away, then quickly glided over to his friends.

Addison lifted the sword as tears rolled down the dreadful looking Duchess's face. Addison, Alistair and the Duchess bowed their heads as each one of them placed their hand on the sword then disappeared, as a cold gray fog filled the room!

The castle began to shake more than ever as books were now falling from the shelves!

"Well, this isn't safe!" said Terrence ducking.

"No kidding, after all of this...I wanna see what's gonna happen!" said Harlo.

They carefully opened the library door and cautiously skated down the hall toward the ominous ballroom.

Forty-five
The Scene of the Crime

Inside the ballroom it was almost like the ghosts were real people! The violent anger seemed to have left them. The ghosts placed the sword in the exact blood stained area and backed away.

Then they just disappeared!

The violent rumbling and shaking of the castle suddenly stopped while Harlo, Terrence, Pal and Donell watched quietly from a far corner near the entrance to the ballroom.

Seconds later, human versions of Addison and Alistair walked into the ballroom! Their clothes were no longer torn or bloodied, but perfectly clean and pressed! They weren't ghosts anymore! They were human!

The dust and cobwebs from the room had vanished, too, as the room changed back to its elegant, original state! It was almost as if they had gone back in time to the 1700s, hundreds of years ago!

"You will stay away from her!" sniped Alistair.

"Why in the good name of Cloon de Sade do you insist on humiliating yourself? When you know perfectly well that it was me she expressed as her heart's desire?" sneered Addison, "and I believe Father knows it."

"Father? Father? He was the one who arranged our meeting! You will die before I let you near her!" screamed Alistair. The two boys continued yelling and screaming at each other at the top of their lungs!

Pal went to say something when Terrence and Donell quickly covered his mouth.

Seconds later, the chandelier with all the crystals began to tremble again. Giant mirrors swayed while the floor began to shake! The wind began to howl and it felt like a tornado, except it was inside the castle! Furniture began sliding around the room as it tilted and swayed while dust swirled and the curtains blew! It felt like the entire castle was coming apart! The team cowered together under the doorway watching the most unbelievable freakish event of their lives!

"ARGUING AGAIN!!!!???" A loud wicked voice boomed as an ominous man with an evil face and a disgusting sneer appeared in the room! He had a black moustache with long curly black hair.

"That's the skeleton guy!" whispered Pal, "I'd know that zombie anywhere!"

The man was wearing a long loose brown suede coat with metal buttons and poufy sleeves with slits in them. He had on breeches to his knees with tall socks and buckle shoes.

It was clear he was the horrible Duke Gregario Cloon de Sade! They shuddered just looking at him!

"This will be the last of it! This is all I can take! I am ruined because of you ungrateful leeches! You have taken away my means to wealth by always arguing and fighting in front of everyone because of your greed! Now I have finally arranged a marriage for one of you, so we may possibly be upstanding and make money again off of her family, and you will not let your competitiveness rest! This is enough!!!"

"But, Father, you set us both up with her," snapped Addison.

"I wasn't sure which one of you she would like best!" snarled the Duke and then he let out a loud wicked laugh as he pulled a sword out of his waistcoat. Addison immediately followed by pulling his sword out of his waistcoat and moving behind the Duke.

The Duke moved toward Alistair, then quickly pivoted away as Addison accidentally plunged his sword into his brother Alistair! Horrified at what he had done, Addison dropped to his knees. When he did, the Duke moved quickly toward him and when Addison went to stand, the Dukes sword impaled his chest! He slumped down over his brother as blood poured onto the marble floor.

Suddenly the Duchess came running into the room. When she saw her boys, she let out the same horrific wail they had heard throughout the castle! She ran over to the Duke and began pounding his chest with her fists! When the Duke tried to hold her back, he hit her in the mouth and she started to bleed!

"Stop!" he screamed, "they've ruined us! They were ungrateful and spoiled and have tarnished our family forever!

"You made them that way!" she screamed and sobbed as she yelled. "You pitted them against each other with your corrupt greed and competitiveness!" You knew if you set them up with the same girl…."

The Duchess grabbed Alistair's sword from his belt. As she went toward the Duke with it, he tried to get the sword from her hand, but she tripped and fell on to the sword that he was wielding!

He stood stunned for a second, then quickly shrugged it off and began rearranging the scene to make it look like it was his horrible sons who had committed the crime!

By the time the Duke had repositioned the bodies to make it look like Alistair had caused the entire thing by fighting with his brother, there were footsteps. Just like hundreds of years ago the Duke took his sword and went to slide the secret ballroom panel open, he was going to leave the ballroom the exact same way he did on the day of the crime!

Only this time it was different! This time he couldn't seem to get the secret panel open! Suddenly, the frightening ghosts of Addison, Alistair, and the Duchess re-emerged!

They began to claw at him, tearing him away from the panel! The castle began rumbling again while dust and again flew around the ballroom as it changed back to the present time.

The team sat frozen, watching in disbelief as the Duchess and the two sons continued tugging on the Duke! The room began to spin! It was like a tornado as everything flew around, including the four ghosts.

Suddenly, a giant black portal opened up right above them! It was filled with lightening flashes and a thick greenish black fog. Tattered empty black robes with hoods twisted around inside the black hole. There was a wicked howling sound.

It began to suck the evil Duke up toward it. He began screaming while he started to turn into black shreds as he was sucked into it! Instantly, the portal closed!

The rumbling and shaking stopped instantly. The evil cold feeling was gone from the room. Addison, Alistair and the Duchess were now beginning to float peacefully. It looked almost like they were sleep walking. Then suddenly three bright beams of light shot through the ceiling hitting

191

each one of them with a jolt! It was so bright that Harlo, Donell, Pal and Terrence had to shield their eyes. Within seconds, the Duchess, Addison and Alistair began to swirl into a frail mist. And in a bright flash of light, they were gone.

The ballroom and the rest of the castle instantly went black, silent and still.

Yet, even though everything was dark, the ominous feeling of dread was gone.

Slowly, Donell, Harlo, Pal and Terrence stood up. Terrence turned the flashlight on and shined it around the room. Nothing was there. He shined it on the portrait above the fireplace. The anger from Addison and Alistair's faces was gone; it was replaced by a calm, serene look, and the Duchess no longer looked sad, but the Duke's face was rubbed out!

Forty-Six
Ghost Talker

They stood there stunned, staring up at the portrait.

"So, that's it?" asked Pal at the exact same moment that Harlo's computer clicked and hummed.

Harlo opened it and read aloud "*...On that fateful day, the Duke, after committing the heinous crime that he had planned, hoisted himself up through his secret pulley that only he knew about. He made his way to the master bedroom to get some of his belongings. The room you were in, where the deceased Duchess had waited for him all these years. The Duke then tiptoed down the stairs, to make his escape. On his way out, he hid his sword in the library desk, just in case anyone caught him, so he couldn't be charged with the crime.*

He knew he would hang in the gallows for such a horrible act, and if it wasn't for that, he was already being sought for numerous counts of fraud, bribery and blackmail in his businesses. He used the peep holes and secret doors he had built into the castle to spy on people at parties. He would eavesdrop on their business dealings and then set them up to blackmail them. He had crookedly obtained most of his wealth. When his twin sons began to take after him with their evil personalities, thanks to what the Duke had taught them, it backfired and began to inhibit their father's social affairs. The Cloon de Sades were shunned from parties and social events. The Duke no longer had a devious means to continue earning his fortune, thus he began to go mad as he instigated the twins even further. He taunted them even more with money and pitted them against each other.

That day, after hiding the sword in the library, the Duke Cloon de Sade heard the servants coming home and left through his secret pulley by lowering himself to his underground dungeon. When all the servants were sleeping, he went out through his escape tunnel. He had already moved his horse to the side of the castle...But his plan backfired when the tunnel wall gave way and he got stuck in mud that had seeped in from underground. His wailing from being caught frightened his horse off the cliff and his servants away from the castle for good! The stories ran rampant. The spirits of the mother and sons could never rest, until now...you have set them free. Thank you. GT"

Just as Harlo finished reading, the computer went black.

"Hey, just who is this GT dude, and where did you get that computer?" insisted Donell.

194

"An electronics store," said Harlo, confused at what GT had just led them through.

Harlo tried to turn the computer on again but with no luck.

"Hey! It's late! We've got a huge demo tomorrow! I'm glad we saved the spirits and all, but my spirit is gonna be broken if we don't get back!" said Pal.

"Yeah, I'm with Pal. Now that we can leave this place…we can worry about what happened here tomorrow," agreed Terrence.

They quietly walked out of the ballroom. There was a whole different vibe to the castle now. They wondered how the Duke had gotten so evil.

"I think it was the money…you know it's the root of all evil! Greed and all that stuff really doesn't get you anywhere," said Donell.

"Yeah, man, all that dude cared about was putting on a show. He was a fake! So he goes mad and broke, then blames it on his misbehaving kids!" said Harlo.

"Glad you guys got it figured out," said Terrence, "but look at this…"

The enormous front door opened easily; and even though it was dark outside they didn't feel afraid. They ran with their boards down the steep hill as fast as they could. When they got to the bottom of the hill, they could see the shadow of the two horses, still tied up to the trees.

They jumped on, and rode them to back to Twickenshire.

"Man, I could've sworn I just saw those lights flick on!" yelled Pal looking back as they galloped away.

"Well, maybe, but if that place is still haunted…those ghosts will have to work it out for themselves!" shouted Harlo.

"Agreed!" hollered Donell as they rode toward the village.

Once there, they tied the horses up behind the pub. They heard a window open above them and Emily poked her head out.

"Thank goodness! I was getting ready to call the police!" she said, "I'll be right down!"

Emily let them into the pub and got them some tea, while Terrence punched in the cab company number on his quad phone. They told her what happened as she jotted down notes. She exchanged emails with Harlo and promised to be in touch.

The 250-year-old mystery had finally been solved.

Forty-Seven
Back to the Hotel

It was late when the cab finally showed up at the pub. During the ride back, they were quiet for awhile thinking about the horrible adventure they had just lived through.

"You gonna keep in touch with GT, bro?" asked Pal, breaking the silence.

"You bet I am…." replied Harlo, "I'm gonna find out who he really is and just why he sent us on that ghost chase!"

"Yeah, I was kinda wonderin' that myself," agreed Donell.

As the cab headed toward London, they continued to quietly discuss the evening's past events.

"I just can't thank you guys enough for showing up!" said Harlo "I probably would've rotted away there forever!"

"Yeah, you probably would've. So next time, let us know where you're going!" said Terrence.

"How did you know where I went?" asked Harlo.

"We just had an idea…we're your posse, bro," replied Pal.

"Hey, I like that - posse. The ghost posse! It's tight!" answered Harlo excitedly.

"Yo…don't forget our boards. If it weren't for them, we wouldn't have ever made it out alive, or solved the mystery," insisted Donell.

"That's true, so we really are The Ghost Board Posse!" stated Harlo.

That was it. They decided the name of their team would be The Ghost Board Posse. They knew they'd have to run it by Ira first. And he would probably hate it, especially since they liked it. It would be easier if they told Brie, maybe she could get it passed through corporate without Ira even having to know.

The cab finally pulled up to their hotel. They were happy and relieved to be back. They knew they had to get some sleep if they were going to be at their skateboarding best for the kickoff of the tour.

But after riding through the haunted castle and dungeon, they felt they had honed their skills and tricks even more!

They warily entered the hotel afraid that Ira's front desk friend, who had tricked them before, might be on duty. They ducked down, and one by one they crept past the front desk then bolted around the corner to the elevators.

Once they got to their floor, they tiptoed to their rooms.

When Terrence entered his room he had to be extra quiet not to wake Ming. He figured they had gotten to a decent level of friendship. Even though there was still something odd about Ming, that Terrence just couldn't figure out. The minute Terrence put his head on the soft pillow and closed his eyes the light clicked on.

"Where have you been?" snapped Ming in his weird voice. "I've been worried sick about you all night!"

"Ming, uh…what are you doing up?" he asked.

"I've been up all night long wondering where you and the rest of your little buddies were! Not one of them were in their rooms! Brie and I had to play musical beds just to keep Ira from finding out you guys had split!"

"Well, don't worry about me or the others. The Ghost Board Posse is back, alive and well," chuckled Terrence in his tired state.

"Ghost Board what? Who the heck is the Ghost Board Posse?" Ming's voice changed.

Terrence sat up, turned and stared at Ming who immediately pulled the covers up over his head, since his hat was on the nightstand.

"Okay, what is up with you, dude? You seem to have secrets of your own and I'm not sharing mine until you tell me yours!" snapped Terrence.

"Keep your voice down," said Ming as she sat up and looked at Terrence. He was shocked to see how

199

different Ming looked without his hat. In fact he was shocked to see – that he was a she!

He was speechless yet relieved, because now he understood the reason why he had cared about what happened to the strange little guy…gal! That he wasn't just some over-caring sap for every single weird or down and out person!

He explained everything; about the castle, the ghosts, freeing the spirits…Ming sat silently with her huge brown eyes wide open staring at Terrence.

Then she explained why she was imitating being a male. That she couldn't land an acting job and this was a chance of a lifetime. She explained how she knew Brie; that they had met on auditions years ago. Luckily, Brie hated Ira enough to join in on the secret.

"Well, you have to admit, like you acted a little odd. I mean, I get it, but you haven't really wowed the others with your dynamic personality!" exclaimed Terrence.

They laughed while deciding that their secrets would have to remain just that until after the tour was over. Terrence turned off the light, and they fell asleep.

Forty-eight
The Tour

The next morning Ira was alone at breakfast until Brie joined him.

"You're late, Cheese!" he barked.

Brie glared at him while squinting her eyes and slamming her briefcase on the table.

"Oh, no! No 'tude from you, my little schlepper. Just where are your boyfriends?' Ira snapped.

"Not my watch today, Ira," Brie sat down exhausted from going room to room the night before covering for them. Ira finally stopped at midnight, so by the time she got to sleep it was late.

"Thank you. I'll just have an orange juice and coffee for now," she said to the waiter.

"I told them to be here promptly at ten," Ira stated. He began to continuously call each one of their phones, hang up and dial again.

"Why aren't you leaving them a message? Plus, they don't have to be at the arena until noon."

"Because I don't want them to get their beauty sleep, that's why, and I know they were up to something last

201

night!" Ira snapped as he began to give Brie his list of orders for the day.

"And don't forget those morons are by no means to ever, ever be interviewed by the press. I'll handle the interviews."

"But you're not the celebrity," she chuckled, knowing instantly that she had overstepped her bounds. But she was saved when the Posse strolled into the dining room.

"Ahhh…will ya just look at who decided to grace us with their presence! If it isn't the Thrash Energy Drink team!"

"Hey, no jokes today Ira. We're tired," said Pal.

"Oh, are you? Now why is that?" Ira questioned.

"And you can call us the Ghost Board Posse from now on," insisted Harlo.

"Says who?" laughed Ira.

They laughed back mimicking his obnoxious laugh. They chatted among themselves using code words, so Ira wouldn't know what they were talking about.

Ira would never find out they had left the hotel. He stood up and began to toss the day's itinerary at each of them. They nodded, thanked him then continued to ignore him.

"If you're late, you won't skate!" Ira snapped as he slammed his briefcase shut and left angrily.

They talked to Brie about getting to a contact to let them use the team name of Ghost Board Posse for the tour. She agreed, but looked at them oddly.

Forty-nine
Ghost Board Posse

As they entered Wembley Arena for the second time, they were again astounded at the masses of people filling the stands. They took their places on the sidelines and began warming up. Although the place was packed, and the event was televised, they no longer felt nervous or afraid.

Even though this was the start of an awesome world tour, the adventure had already begun. After what they had handled the night before, as far as their skating went, they felt that if they could outride ghosts, release spirits, and still make it back in one piece, then the tour would be like skating in a park!

The announcements began as they took their places. Once they started, their riding couldn't have been more perfect. They did some of the most wicked tricks that anyone has ever seen! They all had variations of the Casper that were amazing! Casper disasters, anti-Caspers, Casper flips; they were even pulling big spin flips in unison! On the rails they were pulling dark slides and 360 kick flips to blunt slides on the bench!

But one of the biggest surprises of all was Ming! He took to his board strong, doing pivots as smooth as a dancer, with a grand finale on the vert with a 900! The team was in awe of his skills!

"Wow! Any dude that can skate like that can be a friend of mine!" said Donell.

"No kidding!" said Pal.

"He fits right in!" said Harlo.

"Yeah, Ming will fit in," nodded Terrence, smiling as the rest of the team turned and looked at him strangely.

The tour started with street and wrapped up with one of the tallest vert ramps they had ever skated. Excitement filled the arena!

An hour later the MC began to wrap up the day's successful events. Each one of the team members stepped forward when their name was announced to take a bow. There was a standing ovation from the crowd!

They were so excited they thought they were hearing things when the MC announced, "Give it up! One more time, another round of applause for the fantastic, out of this world Sisu Soda Thrash Energy Drink World Tour, Challenge Yourself Because You'll Be Challenged…GHOST BOARD POSSE!!!"

Again the crowd broke out into thunderous applause, as they began shouting "GHOST BOARD POSSE! GHOST BOARD POSSE!"

The team took one more bow while looking at each other confused. When the MC had said it, they thought for sure they were hearing things…but when the crowd started chanting they were astonished!

They looked at the MC, who was suddenly surrounded by Sisu Soda people. He shrugged his shoulders and looked like he was trying to explain while frantically going through his papers that he had been given to read, as if he was looking for something.

"Brie!" yelled Terrence when he saw her. She joined them in the stands as Terrence asked, "Did you give our new name to the MC?"

"No way! There are some things that I have to run through corporate, and giving you guys a name is one of them," Brie replied.

When the team had taken their last bow, Ira joined them in a fury!

"Who? Who did it? Which one of you is responsible for giving the MC that ridiculous name???!!!" He screamed at them as his face turned bright red and his eyeballs looked like they were going to pop out of their sockets!

They shrugged their shoulders, but were afraid of what would happen with the executives that were now coming their way. Worst of all, the division president of Sisu Soda was walking right behind them!

"Excuse me, Ira," he said sternly, as he forced Ira out of the way and stood right in front of the team. "I do believe it was genius, pure genius! Whoever came up with that Ghost Board Posse name for your excellent Casper tricks! Pure genius! Congrats, blokes! Good luck on the remainder of the tour!" He quickly turned and left.

"Uhhh, excuse me…sir?" Ira followed him.

"Not now, Ira! I must meet with the press. Cheerio!"

Ira was now filled with rage as he turned to talk to the other executives.

The Ghost Board Posse was now officially named, but no one knew who had ordered the announcement. They got in a circle and patted each other on the back. For the Ghost Board Posse, the adventure had just begun!

The Beginning

Photo by Mick Brege

The Breges

Authors, Illustrators, Comedians, Married, Parents, Crazy
& Fun...They love scary stories so here's one for you!

BE A PART OF THE POSSE
visit

www.GHOSTBOARDPOSSE.com